MAGNIFICENT AMBER!

"I envy those who encounter Roger Zelazny!"

Theodore Sturgeon,
The New York Times

"After Tolkien and Donaldson, the most popular fantasy novels of the last few years have been Zelazny's Amber series."

Cleveland Plain Dealer

"Few works of Science Fiction are as satisfying as Zelazny's Amber series. Wickedly crafted and thoroughly engrossing."

Boston Herald

"Daring and magnificent!"
Magazine of Fantasy and Science Fiction

"Zelazny is one of Science Fiction's brightest lights."

Library Journal

Other Avon Books by
Roger Zelazny

CREATURES OF LIGHT AND DARKNESS
THE DOORS OF HIS FACE, THE LAMPS OF HIS MOUTH
DOORWAYS IN THE SAND
LORD OF LIGHT
UNICORN VARIATIONS

The Amber Novels
NINE PRINCES IN AMBER
THE GUNS OF AVALON
SIGN OF THE UNICORN
THE HAND OF OBERON
THE COURTS OF CHAOS
TRUMPS OF DOOM
BLOOD OF AMBER

Coming Soon

THE LAST DEFENDER OF CAMELOT

ROGER ZELAZNY'S VISUAL GUIDE TO CASTLE AMBER
(*An Avon Books Trade Paperback*)
by Roger Zelazny and Neil Randall

ROGER ZELAZNY

SIGN OF CHAOS

AVON BOOKS  NEW YORK

AVON BOOKS
A division of
The Hearst Corporation
105 Madison Avenue
New York, New York 10016

Copyright © 1987 by The Amber Corporation
Cover illustration by Tim White
Published by arrangement with the author
Library of Congress Catalog Card Number: 87-14509
ISBN: 0-380-89637-0

Published in hardcover by Arbor House/William Morrow and Company,
Inc.; for information address Avon Books.

First Avon Books Printing: July 1988

AVON TRADEMARK REG. U.S. PAT. OFF. AND IN OTHER COUNTRIES, MARCA
REGISTRADA, HECHO EN U.S.A.

Printed in the U.S.A.

K-R 10 9 8 7 6 5 4 3 2 1

To Phil Cleverley
and our seasons in the sun:
Thanks for all the *kokyu nages*.

CHAPTER 1

I felt vaguely uneasy, though I couldn't say why. It did not seem all that unusual to be drinking with a White Rabbit, a short guy who resembled Bertrand Russell, a grinning Cat, and my old friend Luke Raynard, who was singing Irish ballads while a peculiar landscape shifted from mural to reality at his back. Well, I was impressed by the huge blue Caterpillar smoking the hookah atop the giant mushroom because I know how hard it is to keep a water pipe lit. Still, that wasn't it. It was a convivial scene, and Luke was known to keep pretty strange company on occasion. So why should I feel uneasy?

The beer was good and there was even a free lunch. The demons tormenting the red-haired woman tied to the stake had been so shiny they'd hurt to look at. Gone now, but the whole thing had been beautiful. Everything was beautiful. When Luke sang of Galway Bay it had been so sparkling and lovely that I'd wanted to dive in and lose myself there. Sad, too.

Something to do with the feeling. . . . Yes. Funny thought. When Luke sang a sad song I felt melancholy. When it was a happy one I was greatly cheered. There seemed an unusual amount of empathy in the air. No matter, I guess. The light show was superb. . . .

I sipped my drink and watched Humpty teeter, there at the end of the bar. For a moment I tried to remember when I'd come into this place, but that cylinder wasn't

1

hitting. It would come to me, eventually. Nice party. . . .

I watched and listened and tasted and felt, and it was all great. Anything that caught my attention was fascinating. Was there something I'd wanted to ask Luke? It seemed there was, but he was busy singing and I couldn't think of it now, anyway.

What had I been doing before I'd come into this place? Trying to recall just didn't seem worth the effort either. Not when everything was so interesting right here and now.

It seemed that it might have been something important, though. Could that be why I felt uneasy? Might it be there was business I had left unfinished and should be getting back to?

I turned to ask the Cat but he was fading again, still seeming vastly amused. It occurred to me then that I, too, could do that. Fade, I mean, and go someplace else. Was that how I had come here and how I might depart? Possibly. I put down my drink and rubbed my eyes and my temples. Things seemed to be swimming inside my head, too.

I suddenly recalled a picture of me. On a giant card. A Trump. Yes. That was how I'd gotten here. Through the card. . . .

A hand fell upon my shoulder and I turned. It belonged to Luke, who grinned at me as he edged up to the bar for a refill.

"Great party, huh?" he said.

"Yeah, great. How'd you find this place?" I asked him.

He shrugged. "I forget. Who cares?"

He turned away, a brief blizzard of crystals swirling between us. The Caterpillar exhaled a purple cloud. A blue moon was rising.

What is wrong with this picture? I asked myself.

I had a sudden feeling that my critical faculty had been shot off in the war, because I couldn't focus on the anomalies I felt must be present. I knew that I was caught up in the moment, but I couldn't see my way clear.

I was caught up. . . .

I was caught. . . .

How?

Well. . . . It had all started when I'd shaken my own hand. No. Wrong. That sounds like Zen and that's not how it was. The hand I shook emerged from the space occupied by the image of myself on the card that went away. Yes, that was it. . . . After a fashion.

I clenched my teeth. The music began again. There came a soft scraping sound near to my hand on the bar. When I looked I saw that my tankard had been refilled. Maybe I'd had too much already. Maybe that's what kept getting in the way of my thinking. I turned away. I looked off to my left, past the place where the mural on the wall became the real landscape. Did that make me a part of the mural? I wondered suddenly.

No matter. If I couldn't think here. . . . I began running . . . to the left. Something about this place was messing with my head, and it seemed impossible to consider the process while I was a part of it. I had to get away in order to think straight, to determine what was going on.

I was across the bar and into that interface area where the painted rocks and trees became three-dimensional. I pumped my arms as I dug in. I heard the wind without feeling it.

Nothing that lay before me seemed any nearer. I was moving, but—

Luke began singing again.

I halted. I turned, slowly, because it sounded as if he were standing practically beside me. He was. I was only a few paces removed from the bar. Luke smiled and kept singing.

"What's going on?" I asked the Caterpillar.

"You're looped in Luke's loop," it replied.

"Come again?" I said.

It blew a blue smoke ring, sighed softly, and said, "Luke's locked in a loop and you're lost in the lyrics. That's all."

"How'd it happen?" I asked.

"I have no idea," it replied.

"Uh, how does one get unlooped?"

"Couldn't tell you that either."

I turned to the Cat, who was coalescing about his grin once again.

"I don't suppose you'd know—" I began.

"I saw him come in and I saw you come in later," said the Cat, smirking. "And even for this place your arrivals were somewhat . . . unusual—leading me to conclude that at least one of you is associated with magic."

I nodded.

"Your own comings and goings might give one pause," I observed.

"I keep my paws to myself," he replied. "Which is more than Luke can say."

"What do you mean?"

"He's caught in a contagious trap."

"How does it work?" I asked.

But he was gone again, and this time the grin went too.

Contagious trap? That seemed to indicate that the problem was Luke's, and that I had been sucked into it in some fashion. This felt right, though it still gave me no idea as to what the problem was or what I might do about it.

I reached for my tankard. If I couldn't solve my problem, I might as well enjoy it. As I took a slow sip I became aware of a strange pair of pale, burning eyes gazing into my own. I hadn't noticed them before, and the thing that made them strange was that they occupied a shadowy corner of the mural across the room from me— that, and the fact that they were moving, drifting slowly to my left.

It was kind of fascinating, when I lost sight of the eyes

but was still able to follow whatever it was from the swaying of grasses as it passed into the area toward which I had been headed earlier. And far, far off to my right—beyond Luke—I now detected a slim gentleman in a dark jacket, palette and brush in hand, who was slowly extending the mural. I took another sip and returned my attention to the progress of whatever it was that had moved from flat reality to 3-D. A gunmetal snout protruded from between a rock and a shrub; the pale eyes blazed above it; blue saliva dripped from the dark muzzle and steamed upon the ground. It was either quite short or very crouched, and I couldn't make up my mind whether it was the entire crowd of us that it was studying or me in particular. I leaned to one side and caught Humpty by the belt or the necktie, whichever it was, just as he was about to slump to the side.

"Excuse me," I said. "Could you tell me what sort of creature that is?"

I pointed just as it emerged—many-legged, long-tailed, dark-scaled, undulating, and fast. Its claws were red, and it raised its tail as it raced toward us.

Humpty's bleary eyes moved toward my own, drifted past.

"I am not here, sir," he began, "to remedy your zoological ignor— My God! It's—"

It flashed across the distance, approaching rapidly. Would it reach a spot shortly where its running would become a treadmill operation—or had that effect only applied to me on trying to get away from this place?

The segments of its body slid from side to side, it hissed like a leaky pressure cooker, and steaming slaver marked its trail from the fiction of paint. Rather than slowing, its speed seemed to increase.

My left hand jerked forward of its own volition and a series of words rose unbidden to my lips. I spoke them just as the creature crossed the interface I had been unable to pierce earlier, rearing as it upset a vacant table and bunching its members as if about to spring.

"A Banderonatch!" someone cried.

"A frumious Bandersnatch!" Humpty corrected.

As I spoke the final word and performed the ultimate gesture, the image of the Logrus swam before my inner vision. The dark creature, having just extended its foremost talons, suddenly drew them back, clutched with them against the upper left quadrant of its breast, rolled its eyes, emitted a soft moaning sound, exhaled heavily, collapsed, fell to the floor, and rolled over onto its back, its many feet extended upward into the air.

The Cat's grin appeared above the creature. The mouth moved.

"A *dead* frumious Bandersnatch," it stated.

The grin drifted toward me, the rest of the Cat occurring about it like an afterthought.

"That was a cardiac arrest spell, wasn't it?" it inquired.

"I guess so," I said. "It was sort of a reflex. Yeah, I remember now. I did still have that spell hanging around."

"I thought so," it observed. "I was sure that there was magic involved in this party."

The image of the Logrus which had appeared to me during the spell's operation had also served the purpose of switching on a small light in the musty attic of my mind. Sorcery. Of course.

I—Merlin, son of Corwin—am a sorcerer, of a variety seldom encountered in the areas I have frequented in recent years. Lucas Raynard—also known as Prince Rinaldo of Kashfa—is himself a sorcerer, albeit of a style different than my own. And the Cat, who seemed somewhat sophisticated in these matters, could well have been correct in assessing our situation as the interior of a spell. Such a location is one of the few environments where my sensitivity and training would do little to inform me as to the nature of my predicament. This, because my faculties would also be caught up in the manifestation and subject to its forces, if the thing were at all self-consistent. It struck me as something similar to color blindness. I could think of no way of telling for certain what was going on, without outside help.

As I mused over these matters, the King's horses and men arrived beyond the swinging doors at the front of the place. The men entered and fastened lines upon the carcass of the Bandersnatch. The horses dragged the thing off. Humpty had climbed down to visit the rest room while this was going on. Upon his return he discovered that he was unable to achieve his former position atop the barstool. He shouted to the King's men to give him a hand, but they were busy guiding the defunct Bandersnatch among tables and they ignored him.

Luke strolled up, smiling.

"So that was a Bandersnatch," he observed. "I'd always wondered what they were like. Now, if we could just get a Jabberwock to stop by—"

"Sh!" cautioned the Cat. "It must be off in the mural somewhere, and likely it's been listening. Don't stir it up! It may come whiffling through the tulgey wood after your ass. Remember the jaws that bite, the claws that catch! Don't go looking for troub—"

The Cat cast a quick glance toward the wall and phased into and out of existence several times in quick succession. Ignoring this, Luke remarked, "I was just thinking of the Tenniel illustration."

The Cat materialized at the far end of the bar, downed the Hatter's drink, and said, "I hear the burbling, and eyes of flame are drifting to the left."

I glanced at the mural, and I, too, saw the fiery eyes and heard a peculiar sound.

"It could be any of a number of things," Luke remarked.

The Cat moved to a rack behind the bar and reached high up on the wall to where a strange weapon hung, shimmering and shifting in shadow. He lowered the thing and slid it along the bar; it came to rest before Luke.

"Better have the Vorpal Sword in hand, that's all I can say."

Luke laughed, but I stared fascinated at the device which looked as if it were made of moth wings and folded moonlight.

Then I heard the burbling again.

"Don't just stand there in uffish thought!" said the Cat, draining Humpty's glass and vanishing again.

Still chuckling, Luke held out his tankard for a refill. I stood there in uffish thought. The spell I had used to destroy the Bandersnatch had altered my thinking in a peculiar fashion. It seemed for a small moment in its aftermath that things were beginning to come clear in my head. I attributed this to the image of the Logrus which I had regarded briefly. And so I summoned it again.

The Sign rose before me, hovered. I held it there. I looked upon it. It seemed as if a cold wind began to blow through my mind. Drifting bits of memory were drawn together, assembled themselves into an entire fabric, were informed with understanding. Of course. . . .

The burbling grew louder and I saw the shadow of the Jabberwock gliding among distant trees, eyes like landing lights, lots of sharp edges for biting and catching. . . .

And it didn't matter a bit. For I realized now what was going on, who was responsible, how and why.

I bent over, leaning far forward, so that my knuckles just grazed the toe of my right boot.

"Luke," I said, "we've got a problem."

He turned away from the bar and glanced down at me.

"What's the matter?" he asked.

Those of the blood of Amber are capable of terrific exertions. We are also able to sustain some pretty awful beatings. So, among ourselves, these things tend to cancel out to some degree. Therefore, one must go about such matters just right if one is to attend to them at all. . . .

I brought my fist up off the floor with everything I had behind it, and I caught Luke on the side of the jaw with a blow that lifted him above the ground as it turned him and sent him sprawling across a table which collapsed, to continue sliding backward the length of the entire serving area where he finally came to a crumpled halt at the feet of the quiet Victorian-looking gentleman—who had dropped his paintbrush and stepped away quickly when Luke came skidding toward him. I raised my tankard with my left hand and poured its contents over my right fist, which felt as if I had just driven it against a mountainside. As I did this the lights grew dim and there was a moment of utter silence.

Then I slammed the mug back onto the bartop. The entire place chose that moment in which to shudder, as if from an earth tremor. Two bottles fell from a shelf, a lamp swayed, the burbling grew fainter. I glanced to my left and saw that the eerie shadow of the Jabberwock had retreated somewhat within the tulgey wood. Not only that, the painted section of the prospect now extended a good deal farther into what had seemed normal space, and it looked to be continuing its advance in that direction, freezing that corner of the world into flat immobility. It became apparent from whiffle to whiffle that the Jabberwock was now moving away, to the left, hurrying ahead of the flatness. Tweedledum, Tweedledee, the Dodo, and the Frog began packing their instruments.

I started across the bar toward Luke's sprawled form. The Caterpillar was disassembling his hookah, and I saw that his mushroom was tilted at an odd angle. The White Rabbit beat it down a hole to the rear, and I heard Humpty muttering curses as he swayed atop the bar stool he had just succeeded in mounting.

I saluted the gentleman with the palette as I approached.

"Sorry to disturb you," I said. "But believe me, this is for the better."

I raised Luke's limp form and slung him over my shoulder. A flock of playing cards flew by me. I drew away from them in their rapid passage.

"Goodness! It's frightened the Jabberwock!" the man remarked, looking past me.

"What has?" I asked, not really certain that I wished to know.

"That," he answered, gesturing toward the front of the bar.

I looked and I staggered back and I didn't blame the Jabberwock a bit.

It was a twelve-foot Fire Angel that had just entered—russet-colored, with wings like stained-glass windows—and, along with intimations of mortality, it brought me recollections of a praying mantis, with a spiked collar and thornlike claws protruding through its short fur at every suggestion of an angle. One of these, in fact, caught on and unhinged a swinging door as it came inside. It was a Chaos beast—rare, deadly, and highly intelligent. I hadn't seen one in years, and I'd no desire to see one now; also, I'd no doubt that I was the reason it was here. For a moment I regretted having wasted my cardiac arrest spell on a mere Bandersnatch—until I recalled that Fire Angels have three hearts. I glanced quickly about as it spied me, gave voice to a brief hunting wail, and advanced.

"I'd like to have had some time to speak with you," I told the artist. "I like your work. Unfortunately—"

"I understand."

"So long."

"Good luck."

I stepped down into the rabbit hole and ran, bent far forward because of the low overhead. Luke made my passage particularly awkward, especially on the turns. I heard a scrabbling noise far to the rear, with a repetition of the hunting wail. I was consoled, however, by the knowledge that the Fire Angel would actually have to enlarge sections of the tunnel in order to get by. The bad news was that it was capable of doing it. The creatures are incredibly strong and virtually indestructible.

I kept running till the floor dipped beneath my feet.

Then I began falling. I reached out with my free hand to catch myself, but there was nothing to catch hold of. The bottom had fallen out. Good. That was the way I'd hoped and half-expected it would be. Luke uttered a single soft moan but did not stir.

We fell. Down, down, down, like the man said. It was a well, and either it was very deep or we were falling very slowly. There was twilight all about us, and I could not discern the walls of the shaft. My head cleared a bit further, and I knew that it would continue to do so for as long as I kept control of one variable: Luke. High in the air overhead I heard the hunting wail once again. It was followed immediately by a strange burbling sound. Frakir began pulsing softly upon my wrist again, not really telling me anything I didn't already know. So I silenced her again.

Clearer yet. I began to remember. . . . My assault on the Keep of the Four Worlds and my recovery of Luke's mother, Jasra. The attack of the werebeast. My odd visit with Vinta Bayle, who wasn't really what she seemed. . . . My dinner in Death Alley. . . . The Dweller, San Francisco, the crystal cave. . . . Clearer and clearer.

. . . And louder and louder the hunting wail of the Fire Angel above me. It must have made it through the tunnel and be descending now. Unfortunately, it possessed wings, while all I could do was fall.

I glanced upward. Couldn't make out its form, though. Things seemed darker up that way than down below. I hoped this was a sign that we were approaching something in the nature of a light at the end of the tunnel, as I couldn't think of any other way out. It was too dark to view a Trump or to distinguish enough of the passing scene to commence a shadow shift.

I felt we were drifting now, rather than falling, at a rate that might permit us to land intact. Should it seem otherwise when we neared the bottom, then a possible means of further slowing our descent came to mind—an adaptation of one of the spells I still carried with me.

However, these considerations were not worth much should we be eaten on the way down—a distinct possibility, unless of course our pursuer were not all that hungry, in which case it might only dismember us. Consequently, it might become necessary to try speeding up to stay ahead of the beast—which of course would cause us to smash when we hit.

Decisions, decisions.

Luke stirred slightly upon my shoulder. I hoped he wasn't about to come around, as I didn't have time to mess with a sleep-spell and I wasn't really in a good position to slug him again. That pretty much left Frakir. But if he were borderline, then choking might serve to rouse him rather than send him back—and I did want him in decent shape. He knew too many things I didn't, things I now needed.

We passed through a slightly brighter area, and I was able to distinguish the walls of the shaft for the first time and to note that they were covered with graffiti in a language that I did not understand. I was reminded of a strange short story by Jamaica Kincaid, but it bore me no clues for deliverance. Immediately following our passage through that band of illumination, I distinguished a small spot of light far below. At almost the same moment I heard the wail once again, this time very near.

I looked up in time to behold the Fire Angel passing through the glow. But there was another shape close behind it, and it wore a vest and burbled. The Jabberwock was also on the way down, and it seemed to be making the best time of any of us. The question of its purpose was immediately prominent; as it gained, the circle of light grew and Luke stirred again. This question was quickly answered, however, as it caught up with the Fire Angel and attacked.

The whiffling, the wailing, and the burbling suddenly echoed down the shaft, along with hissing, scraping, and occasional snarls. The two beasts came together and tore at each other, eyes like dying suns, claws like bayonets, forming a hellish mandala in the pale light which now reached them from below. While this produced a round of activity too near at hand for me to feel entirely at ease, it did serve to slow them to the point where I felt I need not risk an ill-suited spell and an awkward maneuver to emerge from the tunnel in one piece.

"Argh!" Luke remarked, turning suddenly within my grasp.

"I agree," I said. "But lie still, will you? We're about to crash—"

"—and burn," he stated, twisting his head upward to regard the combatant monsters, then downward when he realized that we were falling, too. "What kind of trip is this?"

"A bad one," I answered, and then it hit me: That was exactly what it was.

The opening was even larger now, and our velocity sufficient for a bearable landing. Our reaction to the spell that I called the Giant's Slap would probably slow us to a standstill or even propel us backward. Better to collect a few bruises than become a traffic obstruction at this point.

A bad trip indeed. I was thinking of Random's words as we passed through the opening at a crazy angle, hit dirt, and rolled.

We had come to rest within a cave, near to its mouth. Tunnels ran off to the right and the left. The cave mouth was at my back. A quick glance showed it as opening upon a bright, possibly lush, and more than a little out-of-focus valley. Luke was sprawled unmoving beside me. I got to my feet immediately and caught hold of him beneath the armpits. I began dragging him back away from the dark opening from which we had just emerged. The sounds of the monstrous conflict were very near now.

Good that Luke seemed unconscious again. His condition was bad enough for any Amberite, if my guess were correct. But for one of sorcerous ability it represented a highly dangerous wild card of a sort I'd never encountered before. I wasn't at all certain how I should deal with it.

I dragged him toward the righthand tunnel because it was the smaller of the two and would theoretically be a bit easier to defend. We had barely achieved its shelter when the two beasts fell through the opening, clutching and tearing at each other. They commenced rolling about the floor of the cave, claws clicking, uttering hisses and whistles as they tore at each other. They seemed to have forgotten us entirely, and I continued our retreat until we were well back in the tunnel.

I could only assume Random's guess to be correct. After all, he was a musician and he'd played all over Shadow. Also, I couldn't come up with anything better.

I summoned the Sign of the Logrus. When I had it clear and had meshed my hands with it, I might have used it to strike at the fighting beasts. But they were paying me no heed whatsoever, and I'd no desire to attract their attention. Also, I'd no assurance that the equivalent of being hit by a two-by-four would have much effect on them. Besides, my order was ready, and filling it took precedence.

So I reached.

It took an interminable time. There was an extremely wide area of Shadow to pass through before I found what I was looking for. Then I had to do it again. And again. There were a number of things I wanted, and none of them near.

In the meantime, the combatants showed no sign of slackening, and their claws struck sparks from the cave's walls. They had cut each other in countless places and were now covered with dark gore. Luke had awakened during all of this, propped himself, and was staring fascinated at the colorful conflict. How long it might hold his attention I could not tell. It would be important for me to have him awake very soon now, and I was pleased that he had not started thinking of other matters yet.

I was cheering, by the way, for the Jabberwock. It was

just a nasty beast and need not have been homing in on me in particular when it was distracted by the arrival of its exotic nemesis. The Fire Angel had been playing an entirely different game. There was no reason for a Fire Angel to be stalking about this far from Chaos unless it had been sent. They're devilish hard to capture, harder to train, and dangerous to handle. So they represent a considerable expense and hazard. One does not invest in a Fire Angel lightly. Their main purpose in life is killing, and to my knowledge no one outside the Courts of Chaos has ever employed one. They've a vast array of senses— some of them, apparently, paranormal—and they can be used as Shadow bloodhounds. They don't wander through Shadow on their own, that I know of. But a Shadow-walker can be tracked, and Fire Angels seem to be able to follow a very cold trail once they've been imprinted with the victim's identity. Now, I had been trumped to that crazy bar, and I didn't know they could follow a Trump jump, but several other possibilities occurred to me—including someone's locating me, transporting the thing to my vicinity, and turning it loose to do its business. Whatever the means, though, the attempt had the mark of the Courts upon it. Hence, my quick conversion to Jabberwock fandom.

"What's going on?" Luke asked me suddenly, and the walls of the cave faded for a moment and I heard a faint strain of music.

"It's tricky," I said. "Listen, it's time for your medicine."

I dumped out a palmful of the vitamin B12 tabs I had just brought in and uncapped the water bottle I had also summoned.

"What medicine?" he asked as I passed them to him.

"Doctor's orders," I said. "Get you back on your feet faster."

"Well, okay."

He threw all of them into his mouth and downed them with a single big drink.

"Now these."

I opened the bottle of Thorazine. They were 200 milligrams each and I didn't know how many to give him, so I decided on three. I gave him some tryptophan, too, and some phenylalanine.

He stared at the pills. The walls faded again, the music returned. A cloud of blue smoke drifted past us. Suddenly the bar came into view, back to whatever passed for normal in that place. The upset tables had been righted, Humpty still teetered, the mural went on.

"Hey, the club!" Luke exclaimed. "We ought to head back. Looks like the party's just getting going."

"First, you take your medicine."

"What's it for?"

"You got some bad shit somewhere. This is to let you down easy."

"I don't feel bad. In fact, I feel real good—"

"Take it!"

"Okay! Okay!"

He tossed off the whole fistful.

The Jabberwock and the Fire Angel seemed to be fading now—and my latest exasperated gesture in the vicinity of the bartop had encountered some resistance, though the thing was not fully solid to me yet. Suddenly, then, I noticed the Cat, whose games with substantiality somehow at this point made it seem more real than anything else in the place.

"You coming or going?" it asked.

Luke began to rise. The light grew brighter, though more diffuse.

"Uh, Luke, look over there," I said, pointing.

"Where?" he asked, turning his head.

I slugged him again.

As he collapsed, the bar began to fade. The walls of the cave phased back into focus. I heard the Cat's voice. "Going . . ." it said.

The noises returned full blast, only this time the dominant sound was a bagpipelike squeal. It was coming

from the Jabberwock, who was pinned to the ground and
being slashed at. I decided then to use the Fourth of July
spell I had left over from my assault on the citadel. I
raised my hands and spoke the words. I moved in front
of Luke to block his view as I did so, and I looked away
and squeezed my eyes shut as I said them. Even through
closed eyes I could tell there followed a brilliant flash of
light. I heard Luke say, "Hey!" but all other sounds
ceased abruptly. When I looked again I saw that the two
creatures lay as if stunned, unmoving, toward the far side
of the small cave.

I grabbed hold of Luke's hand and drew him up and
over my shoulders in a fireman's carry. Then I advanced
quickly into the cave, slipping only once on monster
blood as I edged my way along the nearest wall, heading
for the cave mouth. The creatures began to stir before I
made it out, but their movements were more reflexive
than directed. I paused at the opening where I beheld an
enormous flower garden in full bloom. All of the flowers
were at least as tall as myself, and a shifting breeze bore
me an overpowering redolence.

Moments later I heard a more decisive movement at my
back and I turned. The Jabberwock was drawing itself to
its feet. The Fire Angel was still crouched and was
making small piping noises. The Jabberwock staggered
back, spreading its wings, then suddenly turned, beat the
air, and fled back up the high hole in the cleft at the rear
of the cave. Not a bad idea, I decided, as I hurried out
into the garden.

Here the aromas were even stronger, the flowers,
mostly in bloom, a fantastic canopy of colors as I rushed
among them. I found myself panting after a short while,
but I jogged on nevertheless. Luke was heavy, but I
wanted to put as much distance as I could between
ourselves and the cave. Considering how fast our pursuer
could move, I wasn't sure there was sufficient time to fool
with a Trump yet.

As I hurried along I began feeling somewhat woozy,

and my extremities seemed extremely distant. It occurred to me immediately that the flower smells might be a bit narcotic. Great. That was all I needed, to get caught up in a drug high while trying to bring Luke back from one. I could make out a small, slightly elevated clearing in the distance, though, and I headed for it. Hopefully, we could rest there for a bit while I regained my mental footing and decided what to do next. So far, I could detect no sounds of pursuit.

Rushing on, I could feel myself beginning to reel. My equilibrium was becoming impaired. I suddenly felt a fear of falling, almost akin to acrophobia. For it occurred to me that if I fell I might not be able to rise again, that I might succumb to a drugged sleep and be discovered and dispatched by the creature of Chaos while I dozed. Overhead, the colors of the flowers ran together, flowing and tangling like a mass of ribbons in a bright stream. I tried to control my breathing, to take in as little of the effluvia as possible. But this was difficult, as winded as I was becoming.

But I did not fall, though I collapsed beside Luke at the center of the clearing after I'd lowered him to the ground. He remained unconscious, a peaceful expression on his face. A wind swept our hillock from the direction of its far side, where nasty-looking, spiked plants of a nonflowering variety grew. Thus, I no longer smelled the seductive odors of the giant flower field, and after a time my head began to clear. On the other hand, I realized that this meant that our own scents were being borne back in the direction of the cave. Whether the Fire Angel could unmask them within the heady perfumes, I did not know, but providing it with even that much of an opportunity made me feel uncomfortable.

Years ago, as an undergraduate, I had tried some LSD. It had scared me so badly that I'd never tried another hallucinogen since. It wasn't simply a bad trip. The stuff had affected my shadow-shifting ability. It is kind of a truism that Amberites can visit any place they can imagine, for everything is out there, somewhere, in Shadow. By combining our minds with motion we can tune for the shadow we desire. Unfortunately, I could not control what I was imagining. Also unfortunately, I was transported to those places. I panicked, and that only made it worse. I could easily have been destroyed, for I wandered through the objectified jungles of my subconscious and passed some time in places where the bad things dwell. After I came down I found my way back home, turned up whimpering on Julia's doorstep, and was a nervous wreck for days. Later, when I told Random about it, I learned that he had had some similar experiences. He had kept it to himself at first as a possible secret weapon against the rest of the family; but later, after they'd gotten back onto decent terms with each other, he had decided to share the information in the interest of survival. He was surprised to learn then that Benedict, Gérard, Fiona, and Bleys knew all about it—though their knowledge had come from other hallucinogens and, strangely, only Fiona had ever considered its possibility as an in-family weapon. She'd shelved the notion, though, because of its unpredictability. This had been sometime back, however, and in the press of other business in recent years it had slipped his mind; it simply had not occurred to him that a new arrival such as myself should perhaps be cautioned.

Luke had told me that his attempted invasion of the Keep of the Four Worlds, by means of a glider-borne commando team, had been smashed. Since I had seen the broken gliders at various points within the walls during my own visit to that place, it was logical to assume that Luke had been captured. Therefore, it seemed a fairly strong assumption that the sorcerer Mask had done whatever had been done to him to bring him to this state. It would seem that this simply involved introducing a dose of a hallucinogen to his prison fare and turning him loose to wander and look at the pretty lights. Fortunately, unlike myself, his mental travelings had involved nothing more threatening than the brighter aspects of Lewis Carroll. Maybe his heart was purer than mine. But the deal was weird any way you looked at it. Mask might have killed him or kept him in prison or added him to the coatrack collection. Instead, while what had been done was not without risk, it was something which would wear off eventually and leave him chastened but at liberty. It was more a slap on the wrist than a real piece of vengeance. This, for a member of the House which had previously held sway in the Keep and would doubtless like to do so again. Was Mask supremely confident? Or did he not really see Luke as much of a threat?

And then there is the fact that our shadow-shifting abilities and our sorcerous abilities come from similar roots—the Pattern or the Logrus. It had to be that messing with one also messed with the other. That would explain Luke's strange ability to summon me to him as by a massive Trump sending, when in actuality there was no Trump: His drug-enhanced abilities of visualization must have been so intense that the card's physical representation of me was unnecessary. And his skewed magical abilities would account for all of the preliminary byplay, all of the odd, reality-distorting experiences I'd had before he actually achieved contact. This meant that either of us could become very dangerous in certain drugged states. I'd have to remember that. I hoped he wouldn't wake up mad at me for hitting him, before I could talk to him a bit. On the other hand, the tranquilizer would hopefully keep him happy while the other stuff worked at detoxing him.

I massaged a sore muscle in my left leg and rose to my feet. I caught hold of Luke beneath the armpits and dragged him about twenty paces farther along into the clearing. Then I sighed and returned to the spot where I had rested. There was not sufficient time to flee farther. And as the wailing increased in volume and the giant flowers swayed in a line heading directly toward me— glimpses of a darker form becoming visible amid the stalks—I knew that with the Jabberwock fled the Fire Angel was back on the job, and since this confrontation seemed inevitable, this clearing was as good a place to meet it as any, and better than most.

CHAPTER 2

I unfastened the bright thing at my belt and began to unfold it. It made a series of clicking noises as I did so. I was hoping that I was making the best choice available to me rather than, say, a bad mistake.

The creature took longer than I'd thought to pass among the flowers. This could mean it was having trouble following my trail amid its exotic surroundings. I was hoping, though, that it meant it had been sufficiently injured in its encounter with the Jabberwock that it had lost something of its strength and speed.

Whatever, the final stalks eventually swayed and were crushed. The angular creature lurched forward and halted to stare at me with unblinking eyes. Frakir panicked, and I calmed her. This was a little out of her league. I had a Fire Fountain spell left, but I didn't even bother with it. I knew it wouldn't stop the thing, and it might make it behave unpredictably.

"I can show you the way back to Chaos," I shouted, "if you're getting homesick!"

It wailed softly and advanced. So much for sentimentality.

It came on slowly, oozing fluids from a dozen wounds. I wondered if it were still capable of rushing me or if its present pace were the best it could manage. Prudence dictated I assume the worst, so I tried to stay loose and ready to match anything it attempted.

It didn't rush, though. It just kept coming, like a small

tank with appendages. I didn't know where its vital spots
were located. Fire Angel anatomy had not been high on
my list of interests back home. I gave myself a crash
course, however, in the way of gross observation as it
approached. Unfortunately, this gave me to believe that it
kept everything important well protected. Too bad.

I did not want to attack in case it was trying to sucker
me into something. I was not aware of its combat tricks,
and I did not care to expose myself unduly in order to
learn them. Better to stay on the defense and let it make
the first move, I told myself. But it just kept moving
nearer and nearer. I knew that I'd be forced to do
something soon, even if it were only to retreat. . . .

One of those long, folded front appendages flashed out
toward me, and I spun to the side and cut. Snicker-snack!
The limb lay on the ground, still moving. So I kept
moving, also. One-two, one-two! Snicker-snack!

The beast toppled slowly to its left, for I had removed
all of the limbs on that side of its body.

Then, overconfident, I passed too near in racing to
round its head to reach the other side and repeat the
performance while it was still traumatized and collapsing.
Its other extensor flashed out. But I was too near and it
was still toppling. Instead of catching me with its clawed
extremity, it hit me with the equivalent of shin or
forearm. The blow struck me across the chest and I was
knocked backward.

As I scrambled away and drew my feet beneath me to
rise, I heard Luke say, groggily, "Now what's going
on?"

"Later," I called, without looking back.

Then, "Hey! You hit me!" he added.

"All in good fun," I answered. "Part of the cure,"
and I was up and moving again.

"Oh," I heard him say.

The thing was on its side now and that big limb struck
wildly at me, several times. I avoided it and was able to
gauge its range and striking angle.

Snicker-snack The limb fell to the ground and I moved in.

I swung three blows which passed all the way through its head from different angles before I was able to sever it. It kept making clicking noises, though, and the torso kept pitching and scrabbling about on the remaining limbs.

I don't know how many times I struck after that. I just kept at it until the creature was literally diced. Luke had begun shouting "Olé!" each time that I struck. I was perspiring somewhat by then, and I noticed that heat waves or something seemed to be causing my view of the distant flowers to ripple in a disturbing fashion. I felt foresighted as all hell, though—the Vorpal Sword I'd appropriated back in the bar had proved a fine weapon. I swung it through a high arc, which I'd noted seemed to cleanse it entirely, and then I began folding it back into its original compact form. It was as soft as flower petals, and it still gave off a faint dusty glow. . . .

"Bravo!" said a familiar voice, and I turned until I saw the smile followed by the Cat, who was tapping his paws lightly together. "Callooh! Callay!" he added. "Well done, beamish boy!"

The background wavering grew stronger, and the sky darkened. I heard Luke say "Hey!" and when I glanced back I saw him getting to his feet, moving forward. When I looked again I could see the bar forming at the Cat's back, and I caught a glimpse of the brass rail. My head began to swim.

"There's normally a deposit on the Vorpal Sword," the Cat was saying. "But since you're returning it intact—"

Luke was beside me. I could hear music again, and he was humming along with it. Now it was the clearing, with its butchered Fire Angel, that seemed the superimposition, as the bar increased in solidity, taking on nuances of color and shading.

But the place seemed somehow smaller—the tables closer together, the music softer, the mural more

compressed and its artist out of sight. Even the Caterpillar and his mushroom had retreated to a shadowy nook,
and both seemed shrunken, the blue smoke less dense. I
took this as a vaguely good sign, for if our presence there
were a result of Luke's state of mind then perhaps the
fixation was losing its hold on him.

"Luke?" I said.

He moved up to the bar beside me.

"Yeah?" he answered.

"You know you're on a trip, don't you?"

"I don't. . . . I'm not sure what you mean," he said.

"When Mask had you prisoner I think he slipped you
some acid," I said. "Is that possible?"

"Who's Mask?" he asked me.

"The new head honcho at the Keep."

"Oh, you mean Sharu Garrul," he said. "I do
remember that he had on a blue mask."

I saw no reason to go into an explanation as to why
Mask wasn't Sharu. He'd probably forget, anyway. I just
nodded and said, "The boss."

"Well . . . yes, I guess he could have given me
something," he replied. "You mean that all this . . . ?"
He gestured toward the room at large.

I nodded.

"Sure, it's real," I said. "But we can transport
ourselves into hallucinations. They're all real somewhere.
Acid'll do it."

"I'll be damned," he said.

"I gave you some stuff to bring you down," I told
him. "But it may take a while."

He licked his lips and glanced about.

"Well, there's no hurry," he said. Then he smiled as
a distant screaming began and the demons started in doing
nasty things to the burning woman off in the mural. "I
kind of like it here."

I placed the folded weapon back upon the bartop. Luke
rapped on the surface beside it and called for another
round of brews. I backed away, shaking my head.

"I've got to go now," I told him. "Someone's still after me, and he just came close."

"Animals don't count," Luke said.

"The one I just chopped up does," I answered. "It was sent."

I looked at the broken doors, wondering what might come through them next. Fire Angels have been known to hunt in pairs.

"But I've got to talk to you . . . ," I continued.

"Not now," he said, turning away.

"You know it's important."

"I can't think right," he answered.

I supposed that had to be true, and there was no sense trying to drag him back to Amber or anywhere else. He'd just fade away and show up here again. His head would have to clear and his fixation dissipate before we could discuss mutual problems.

"You remember that your mother is a prisoner in Amber?" I asked.

"Yes."

"Call me when you've got your head together. We have to talk."

"I will."

I turned away and walked out the doors and into a bank of fog. In the distance I heard Luke begin singing again, some mournful ballad. Fog is almost as bad as complete darkness when it comes to shadow-shifting. If you can't see any referents while you're moving, there is no way to use the ability that allows you to slip away. On the other hand, I just wanted to be alone for a time to think, now my head was clear. If I couldn't see anybody in this stuff, nobody could see me either. And there were no sounds other than my own footfalls on a cobbled surface.

So what had I achieved? When I was awakened from a brief nap to attend Luke's unusual sending to Amber, I'd been dead tired following extraordinary exertions. I was transported into his presence, learned that he was tripping, fed him something I hoped would bring him off it sooner, hacked up a Fire Angel, and left Luke back where he had started.

I'd gotten two things out of it, I mused, as I strolled through the cottony mist: I'd stalemated Luke in any designs he might still have upon Amber. He was now aware that his mother was our prisoner, and I couldn't see him bringing any direct action against us under the circumstances. Aside from the technical problems involved in transporting Luke and keeping him in one place, this was the reason I was willing to leave him as I just had. I'm sure Random would have preferred him unconscious in a cell in the basement, but I was certain he would settle for a defanged Luke at large; especially so, when it was likely that Luke would be getting in touch with us sooner or later regarding Jasra. I was willing to let him come down and come around in his own good time. I had problems of my own in the waiting room, like Ghostwheel, Mask, Vinta . . . and the new specter which had just taken a number and a seat.

Maybe it had been Jasra who had been using the homing power of the blue stones to send assassins after me. She had the ability as well as a motive. It could also have been Mask, though, who I'd judge had the ability— and who seemed to have a motive, though I didn't understand it. Jasra was out of the way now, however; and while I intended to have things out with Mask eventually, I believed that I had succeeded in detuning myself from the blue stones. I also believed that I might have scared Mask somewhat in our recent encounter at the Keep. Whatever, it was extremely unlikely that Mask or Jasra, whatever their powers, would have had access to a trained Fire Angel. No, there's only one place Fire Angels come from, and shadow-sorcerers aren't on the customer list.

A puff of wind parted the fog for a moment and I caught sight of dark buildings. Good. I shifted. The fog moved again almost immediately, and they were not buildings but dark rock formations. Another parting and a piece of dawn or evening sky came into view, a foam of bright stars spilled across it. Before too long a wind whipped the fog away and I saw that I walked in a high rocky place, the heavens a blaze of starry light bright enough to read by. I followed a dark trail leading off to the edge of the world. . . .

The whole business with Luke, Jasra, Dalt, and Mask was somehow of a piece—completely understandable in some places and clouded in others. Given some time and legwork it would all hang together. Luke and Jasra seemed to be nullified now. Mask, an enigma of sorts, seemed to have it in for me personally but did not appear to represent any particular threat to Amber. Dalt, on the other hand, did, with his fancy new weaponry—but Random was aware of this situation and Benedict was back in town. So I was confident that everything possible was being done to deal with this.

I stood at the edge of the world and looked down into a bottomless rift full of stars. My mountain did not seem to grace the surface of a planet. However, there was a bridge to my left, leading outward to a dark, star-occluding shape—another floating mountain, perhaps. I strolled over and stepped out onto the span. Problems involving atmosphere, gravitation, temperature, meant nothing here, where I could, in a sense, make up reality as I went along. I walked out onto the bridge, and for a moment the angle was right and I caught a glimpse of another bridge on the far side of the dark mass, leading off to some other darkness.

I halted in the middle, able to see along it for a great distance in either direction. It seemed a safe and appropriate spot. I withdrew my packet of Trumps and riffled through them until I located one I hadn't used in a long, long time.

I held it before me and put the others away, studying the blue eyes and the young, hard, slightly sharp features beneath a mass of pure white hair. He was dressed all in black, save for a bit of white collar and sleeve showing beneath the glossy tight-fitting jacket. He held three dark steel balls in his gloved hand.

Sometimes it's hard to reach all the way to Chaos, so I focused and extended, carefully, strongly. The contact came almost immediately. He was seated on a balcony beneath a crazily stippled sky, the Shifting Mountains sliding to his left. His feet were propped on a small floating table and he was reading a book. He lowered it and smiled faintly.

"Merlin," he said softly. "You look tired."

I nodded.

"You look rested," I said.

"True," he answered, as he closed the book and set it on the table. Then, "There is trouble?" he asked.

"There is trouble, Mandor."

He rose to his feet.

"You wish to come through?"

I shook my head. "If you have any Trumps handy for getting back, I'd rather you came to me."

He extended his hand.

"All right," he said.

I reached forward, our hands clasped; he took a single step and stood beside me on the bridge. We embraced for a moment and then he turned and looked out and down into the rift.

"There is some danger here?" he asked.

"No. I chose this place because it seems very safe."

"Scenic, too," he replied. "What's been happening to you?"

"For years I was merely a student, and then a designer of certain sorts of specialized machinery," I told him. "Things were pretty uneventful until fairly recently. Then all hell broke loose—but most of it I understand, and much of it seems under control. That part's complicated and not really worth your concern."

He rested a hand on the bridge's side-piece.

"And the other part?" he asked.

"My enemies up until this point had been from the

cnvirons of Amber. But suddenly, when it seemed that most of that business was on its way to being settled, someone put a Fire Angel on my trail. I succeeded in destroying it just a little while ago. I've no idea why, and it's certainly not an Amber trick.''

He made a clicking noise with his lips as he turned away, paced a few steps, and turned back.

"You're right, of course," he said. "I'd no idea it had come anywhere near this, or I'd have spoken with you some time ago. But let me differ with you as to orders of importance before I indulge in certain speculations on your behalf. I want to hear your entire story.''

"Why?"

"Because you are sometimes appallingly naive, little brother, and I do not yet trust your judgment as to what is truly important.''

"I may starve to death before I finish," I answered.

Smiling crookedly, my step-brother Mandor raised his arms. While Jurt and Despil are my half-brothers, borne by my mother, Jasra, to Prince Sawall the Rim Lord, Mandor was Sawall's son by an earlier marriage. Mandor is considerably older than I, and as a result he reminds me much of my relatives back in Amber. I'd always felt a bit of an outsider among the children of Dara and Sawall. In that Mandor was—in a more stable sense—not part of that particular grouping either, we'd had something in common. But whatever the impulse behind his early attentions, we'd hit it off and become closer, I sometimes think, than full blood brothers. He had taught me a lot of practical things over the years, and we had had many good times together.

The air was distorted between us, and when Mandor lowered his arms a dinner table covered with embroidered white linen came into sudden view between us, soundlessly, followed a moment later by a pair of facing chairs. The table bore numerous covered dishes, fine china, crystal, silverware; there was even a gleaming ice bucket with a dark twisted bottle within it.

"I am impressed," I stated.

"I've devoted considerable time to gourmet magic in recent years," he said. "Pray, be seated."

We made ourselves comfortable there on the bridge between two darknesses. I muttered appreciatively as I tasted, and it was some minutes before I could begin a summary of the events that had brought me to this place of starlight and silence.

Mandor listened to my entire tale without interruption, and when I'd finished he nodded and said, "Would you care for another serving of dessert?"

"Yes," I agreed. "It's quite nice."

When I glanced up a few moments later, I saw that he was smiling.

"What's funny?" I asked.

"You," he replied. "If you recall, I told you before you left for that place to be discriminating when it came to giving your trust."

"Well? I told no one my story. If you're going to lecture me on being friendly with Luke without learning his, I've already heard it."

"And what of Julia?"

"What do you mean? She never learned. . . ."

"Exactly. And she seems like one you could have trusted. Instead, you turned her against you."

"All right! Maybe I used bad judgment there, too."

"You designed a remarkable machine, and it never occurred to you it might also become a potent weapon. Random saw that right away. So did Luke. You might have been saved from disaster on that front only by the fact that it became sentient and didn't care to be dictated to."

"You're right. I was more concerned with solving technical problems. I didn't think through all the consequences."

He sighed.

"What am I going to do with you, Merlin? You take risks when you don't even know you're taking risks."

"I didn't trust Vinta," I volunteered.

"I think you could have gotten more information out of her," he said, "if you hadn't been so quick to save Luke, who already appeared to be out of danger. She seemed to be loosening up considerably at the end of your dialogue."

"Perhaps I should have called you."

"If you encounter her again, do it, and I'll deal with her."

I stared. He seemed to mean it.

"You know what she is?"

"I'll unriddle her," he said, swirling the bright orange beverage in his glass. "But I've a proposal for you, elegant in its simplicity. I've a new country place, quite secluded, with all the amenities. Why not return to the Courts with me rather than bouncing around from hazard to hazard? Lie low for a couple of years, enjoy the good life, catch up on your reading. I'll see that you're well protected. Let everything blow over, then go about your business in a more peaceful climate."

I took a small sip of the fiery drink.

"No," I said. "What happened to those things you indicated earlier that you knew and I didn't?"

"Hardly important, if you accept my offer."

"Even if I were to accept, I'd want to know."

"Bag of worms," he said.

"You listened to my story. I'll listen to yours."

He shrugged and leaned back in his chair, looked up at stars.

"Swayvill is dying," he said.

"He's been doing that for years."

"True, but he's gotten much worse. Some think it has to do with the death curse of Eric of Amber. Whatever, I really believe he hasn't much longer."

"I begin to see. . . ."

"Yes, the struggle for the succession has become more

intense. People have been falling over left and right—poison, duels, assassinations, peculiar accidents, dubious suicides. A great number have also departed for points unknown. Or so it would seem."

"I understand, but I don't see where it concerns me."

"One time it would not have."

"But?"

"You are not aware that Sawall adopted you, formally, after your departure?"

"What?"

"Yes. I was never certain as to his exact motives. But you are a legitimate heir. You follow me but take precedence over Jurt and Despil."

"That would still leave me way in hell down on the list."

"True," he said slowly. "Most of the interest lies at the top. . . ."

"You say 'most.' "

"There are always exceptions," he answered. "You must realize that a time such as this is also a fine occasion for the paying off of old debts. One death more or less hardly rouses an eyebrow the way it would have in more placid times. Even in relatively high places."

I shook my head as I met his eyes.

"It really doesn't make sense in my case," I said.

He continued to stare until I felt uncomfortable.

"Does it?" I finally asked.

"Well . . ." he said. "Give it some thought."

I did. And just as the notion came to me, Mandor nodded as if he viewed the contents of my mind.

"Jurt," he said, "met the changing times with a mixture of delight and fear. He was constantly talking of the latest deaths and of the elegance and apparent ease with which some of them were accomplished. Hushed tones interspersed with a few giggles. His fear and his desire to increase his own capacity for mischief finally reached a point where they became greater than his other fear—"

''The Logrus. . . .''

''Yes. He finally tried the Logrus, and he made it through.''

''He should be feeling very good about that. Proud. It was something he'd wanted for years.''

''Oh, yes,'' Mandor answered. ''And I'm sure he felt a great number of other things as well.''

''Freedom,'' I suggested. ''Power,'' and as I studied his half-amused expression, I was forced to add, ''and the ability to play the game himself.''

''There may be hope for you,'' he said. ''Now, would you care to carry that through to its logical conclusion?''

''Okay,'' I responded, thinking of Jurt's left ear as it floated away following my cut, a swarm of blood-beads spreading about it. ''You think Jurt sent the Fire Angel.''

''Most likely,'' he replied. ''But would you care to pursue that a little further?''

I thought of the broken branch piercing Jurt's eyeball as we wrestled in the glade. . . .

''All right,'' I said. ''He's after me. It could be a part of the succession game, because I'm slightly ahead of him on that front, or just plain dislike and revenge—or both.''

''It doesn't really matter which,'' Mandor said, ''in terms of results. But I was thinking of that crop-eared wolf that attacked you. Only had one eye, too, it seemed. . . .''

''Yes,'' I said. ''What does Jurt look like these days?''

''Oh, he's grown about half the ear back. It's pretty ragged and ugly-looking. Generally, his hair covers it. The eyeball is regenerated, but he can't see out of it yet. He usually wears a patch.''

''That might explain recent developments,'' I said. ''Hell of a time for it, though, with everything else that's been going on. Muddies the waters considerably.''

''It's one of the reasons I suggest you simply drop out and let everything cool down. Too busy. With as many arrows as there seem to be in the air, one may well find your heart.''

"I can take care of myself, Mandor."

"You could have fooled me."

I shrugged, got up, walked over to the rail, and looked down at the stars.

After a long while he called out to me, "Have you got any better ideas?" but I didn't answer him because I was thinking about that very matter. I was considering what Mandor had said about my tunnel vision and lack of preparedness and had just about concluded that he was right, that in nearly everything that had happened to me up to this point—with the exception of my going after Jasra—I had mainly been responding to circumstance. I had been far more acted upon than acting. Admittedly, it had all happened very quickly. But still, I had not formed any real plans for covering myself, learning about my enemies or striking back. It seemed that there were some things I might be doing. . . .

"If there is that much to worry about," he said, "you are probably better off playing it safe."

He was probably right, from the standpoints of reason, safety, caution. But he was strictly of the Courts, while I possessed an additional set of loyalties in which he did not participate. It was possible—if only through my connection with Luke—that I might be able to come up with some personal course of action that would further the security of Amber. So long as such a chance existed, I felt obliged to pursue matters. And beyond this, from a purely personal standpoint, my curiosity was too strong to permit me to walk away from the unanswered questions which abounded when I could be actively seeking some answers.

As I was considering how I might best phrase these matters in my reply to Mandor, I was again acted upon. I became aware of a faint feeling of inquiry, as of a cat scratching at the doors of my mind. It grew in force, thrusting aside other considerations, until I knew it as a Trump sending from some very distant place. I guessed that it might be from Random, anxious to discover what had transpired since my absence from Amber. So I made myself receptive, inviting the contact.

"Merlin, what's the matter?" Mandor asked, and I raised my hand to indicate I was occupied. At that, I saw him place his napkin upon the tabletop and rise to his feet.

My vision cleared slowly and I beheld Fiona, looking stern, rocks at her back, a pale green sky above her.

"Merlin," she said. "Where are you?"

"Far away," I answered. "It's a long story. What's going on? Where are you?"

She smiled bleakly.

"Far away," she replied.

"We seem to have chosen very scenic spots," I observed. "Did you pick the sky to complement your hair?"

"Enough!" she said. "I did not call you to compare travel notes."

At that moment Mandor came up beside me and placed his hand upon my shoulder, which was hardly in keeping with his character, as it is considered a gauche thing to do when a Trump communication is obviously in progress—on the order of intentionally picking up an extension phone and breaking in on someone's call. Nevertheless. . . .

"My! My!" he said. "Will you please introduce me, Merlin?"

"Who," Fiona asked, "is that?"

"This is my brother Mandor," I told her, "of the House of Sawall in the Courts of Chaos. Mandor, this is my Aunt Fiona, Princess of Amber."

Mandor bowed.

"I have heard of you, Princess," he said. "It is indeed a pleasure."

Her eyes widened for a moment.

"I know of the house," she replied, "but I'd no idea of Merlin's relationship with it. I am pleased to know you."

"I take it there's some problem, Fi?" I asked.

"Yes," she answered, glancing at Mandor.

"I will retire," he said. "Honored to have met you, Princess. I wish you lived a bit nearer the Rim."

She smiled.

"Wait," she said. "This does not involve any state secrets. You are an initiate of the Logrus?"

"I am," he stated.

". . . And I take it you two did not get together to fight a duel?"

"Hardly," I answered.

"In that case, I would welcome his view of the problem, also. Are you willing to come to me, Mandor?"

He bowed again, which I thought was hamming it a bit.

"Anyplace, Madam," he responded.

She said, "Come then," and she extended her left hand and I clasped it. Mandor reached out and touched her wrist. We stepped forward.

We stood before her in the rocky place. It was breezy and a bit chill there. From somewhere distant there came a muted roar, as of a muffled engine.

"Have you been in touch with anyone in Amber recently?" I asked her.

"No," she stated.

"Your departure was somewhat abrupt."

"There were reasons."

"Such as your recognizing Luke?"

"His identity is known to you now?"

"Yes."

"And to the others?"

"I told Random," I answered, "and Flora."

"Then everyone knows," she said. "I departed quickly and took Bleys with me because we had to be next on Luke's list. After all, I tried killing his father and almost succeeded. Bleys and I were Brand's closest relatives, and we'd turned against him."

She turned a penetrating gaze upon Mandor, who smiled.

"I understand," he stated, "that right now Luke drinks with a Cat, a Dodo, a Caterpillar, and a White Rabbit. I also understand that with his mother a prisoner in Amber he is powerless against you."

She regarded me again.

"You *have* been busy," she said.

"I try."

". . . So that it is probably safe for you to return," Mandor continued.

She smiled at him, then glanced at me.

"Your brother seems well informed," she observed.

"He's family, too," I said, "and we've a lifelong habit of looking out for each other."

"His life or yours?" she asked.

"Mine," I replied. "He *is* my senior."

"What are a few centuries this way or that?" Mandor offered.

"I thought I felt a certain maturity of spirit," she noted. "I've a mind to trust you further than I'd intended."

"That's very sporting of you," he replied, "and I treasure the sentiment. . . ."

". . . But you'd rather I didn't overdo it?"

"Precisely."

"I've no intention of testing your loyalties to home and throne," she said, "on such short acquaintance. It does concern both Amber and the Courts, but I see no conflict in the matter."

"I do not doubt your prudence. I merely wanted to make my position clear."

She turned back toward me.

"Merlin," she said then, "I think you lied to me."

I felt myself frowning as I tried to recall an occasion when I might have misled her about something. I shook my head.

"If I did," I told her, "I don't remember."

"It was some years ago," she said, "when I asked you to try walking your father's Pattern."

"Oh," I answered, feeling myself blush and wondering whether it was apparent in this strange light.

"You took advantage of what I had told you—about the Pattern's resistance," she continued. "You pretended it was preventing you from setting your foot upon it. But there was no visible sign of the resistance, such as there was when I tried stepping onto it."

She looked at me, as if for confirmation.

"So?" I said.

"So," she replied, "it has become more important now than it was then, and I have to know: Were you faking it that day?"

"Yes," I said.

"Why?"

"Once I took one step upon it," I explained, "I'd have been committed to walking it. Who knows where it might have led me and what situation might have followed? I was near the end of my holiday and in a hurry to get back to school. I didn't have time for what might have turned into a lengthy expedition. Telling you there were difficulties seemed the most graceful way of begging off."

"I think there's more to it than that," she said.

"What do you mean?"

"I think Corwin told you something about it that the rest of us do not know—or that he left you a message. I believe you know more than you let on concerning the thing."

I shrugged.

"Sorry, Fiona. I have no control over your suspicions," I said. "Wish I could be of more help."

"You can," she replied.

"Tell me how."

"Come with me to the place of the new Pattern. I want you to walk it."

I shook my head.

"I've got a lot more pressing business," I told her,

"than satisfying your curiosity about something my dad did years ago."

"It's more than just curiosity," she said. "I told you once before that I think it's what is behind the increased incidence of shadow storms."

"And I gave you a perfectly good reason for something else being the cause. I believe it's an adjustment to the partial destruction and recreation of the old Pattern."

"Would you come this way?" she asked, and she turned from me and began to climb.

I glanced at Mandor, shrugged, and followed her. He came along.

We mounted toward a jagged screen of rock. She reached it first and made her way onto a lopsided ledge which ran partway along it. She traversed this until she came to a place where the rock wall had broken down into a wide V-shaped gap. She stood there with her back to us then, the light from the green sky doing strange things to her hair.

I came up beside her and followed the direction of her gaze. On a distant plain, far below us and to the left, a large black funnel spun like a top. It seemed the source of the roaring sound we had been hearing. The ground appeared to be cracked beneath it. I stared for several minutes, but it did not change in form or position. Finally, I cleared my throat.

"Looks like a big tornado," I said, "not going anyplace."

"That's why I want you to walk the new Pattern," she told me. "I think it's going to get us unless we get it first."

CHAPTER 3

If you had a choice between the ability to detect false-hood and the ability to discover truth, which one would you take? There was a time when I thought they were different ways of saying the same thing, but I no longer believe that. Most of my relatives, for example, are almost as good at seeing through subterfuge as they are at perpetrating it. I'm not at all sure, though, that they care much about truth. On the other hand, I'd always felt there was something noble, special, and honorable about seeking truth—a thing I'd attempted with Ghostwheel. Mandor had made me wonder, though. Had this made me a sucker for truth's opposite?

Of course, it's not as cut and dried as all that. I know that it is not a pure either/or situation with the middle excluded, but is rather a statement of attitude. Still, I was suddenly willing to concede that I might have gone to an extreme—to the point of foolhardiness—and that I had let certain of my critical faculties doze for far too long.

So I wondered about Fiona's request.

"What makes it such a threat?" I asked her.

"It is a shadow storm in the form of a tornado," she said.

"There have been such things before," I answered.

"True," she responded, "but they tend to move through Shadow. This one does have extension through an area of Shadow, but it is totally stationary. It first appeared several days ago, and it has not altered in any way since then."

"What's that come to in Amber-time?" I asked.

"Half a day, perhaps. Why?"

I shrugged. "I don't know. Just curious," I said. "I still don't see why it's a threat."

"I told you that such storms had proliferated since Corwin drew the extra Pattern. Now they're changing in character as well as frequency. That Pattern has to be understood soon."

A moment's quick reflection showed me that whoever gained control of Dad's Pattern could become master of some terrible forces. Or mistress.

So, "Supposing I walk it," I said. "Then what? As I understand it from Dad's story, I'd just wind up in the middle, the same as with the Pattern back home. What's to be learned from that?"

I studied her face for some display of emotion, but my relatives tend to have too much control for such simple self-betrayal.

"As I understand it," she said, "Brand was able to trump in when Corwin was at the middle."

"That's the way I understand it, too."

". . . So, when you reach the center, I can come in on a Trump."

"I suppose so. Then there will be two of us standing at the middle of the Pattern."

". . . And from there we will be in a position to go someplace we could not reach from any other point in existence."

"That being?" I asked.

"The primal Pattern which lies behind it."

"You're sure there is one?"

"There must be. It is in the nature of such a construct to be scribed at a more basic level of reality as well as the mundane."

"And our purpose in traveling to that place?"

"That is where its secrets dwell, where its deepest magics might be learned."

"I see," I told her. "Then what?"

"Why, there we might learn how to undo the trouble the thing is causing," she answered.

"That's all?"

Her eyes narrowed.

"We will learn whatever we can, of course. Power is power, and represents a threat until it is understood."

I nodded slowly.

"But right now there are a number of powers that are more pressing in the threat department," I said. "That Pattern is going to have to wait its turn."

"Even if it may represent the forces you need to deal with your other problems?" she asked.

"Even so," I said. "It might turn into a lengthy enterprise, and I don't believe I have the time for that."

"But you don't know that for certain."

"True. But once I set foot on it, there's no turning back."

I did not add that I'd no intention of taking her to the primal Pattern, then leaving her there on her own. After all, she had tried her hand at king-making once. And if Brand had made it to the throne of Amber in those days, she would have been standing right behind him, no matter what she had to say about it now. I think she was about to ask me to deliver her to the primal Pattern then but realized that I'd already considered it and rejected it. Not wanting to lose face by asking and being refused, she returned to her original argument.

"I suggest you make time now," she said, "if you do not wish to see worlds torn up about you."

"I didn't believe you the first time you told me that," I answered, "and I don't believe you now. I still think the increased shadow-storm activity is probably an adjustment to the damage and repair of the original Pattern. I also think that if we mess around with a new Pattern we don't know anything about, we stand a chance of making things worse, not better—''

"I don't want to mess around with it," she said. "I want to study—''

The Sign of the Logrus flashed between us suddenly. She must have seen it or felt it somehow, too, because she drew back at the same instant I did.

I turned my head with sure knowledge as to what I would see.

Mandor had mounted the battlementlike wall of stone. He stood as still as if he were a part of it, his arms upraised. I suppressed my first impulse, which was to shout to him to stop. He knew what he was doing. And I was certain that he would not pay me the slightest heed, anyway.

I advanced to the notch in which he had taken his position, and I looked past him at the swirling thing on the cracked plain far below. Through the image of the Logrus, I felt the dark, awful rush of power that Suhuy had revealed to me in his final lesson. Mandor was calling upon it now and pouring it into the shadow-storm. Did he not realize that the force of Chaos he was unleashing must spread until it had run a terrible course? Could he not see that if the storm were indeed a manifestation of Chaos then he was turning it into a truly monstrous thing?

It grew larger. Its roaring increased in volume. It became frightening to watch it.

From behind me, I heard Fiona gasp.

"I hope you know what you're doing," I called to him.

"We'll know in about a minute," he replied, lowering his arms.

The Sign of the Logrus winked out before me.

We watched the damned thing spin for some time, bigger and noisier.

Finally, "What have you proved?" I asked him.

"That you have no patience," he answered.

There was nothing particularly instructive to the phenomenon, but I continued to watch it anyway.

Abruptly, the sound became a stutter. The dark apparition jerked about suddenly, shaking off bits of accumulated debris as it contracted. Soon it was restored to its former size, and it hit its earlier pitch and the sound grew steady once more.

"How did you do that?" I asked him.

"I didn't," he said. "It adjusted itself."

"It shouldn't have," Fiona stated.

"Exactly," he replied.

"You've lost me," I said.

"It should have gone roaring right on, stronger than ever, after he'd augmented it that way," Fiona said. "But whatever is controlling it had other plans. So it was readjusted."

". . . And it is a Chaos phenomenon," Mandor continued. "You could see that in the way it drew upon Chaos when I provided the means. But that pushed it past some limit, and there was a correction. Someone is playing with the primal forces themselves out there. Who or what or why, I cannot say. But I think it's strong testimony that the Pattern isn't involved. Not with Chaos games. So Merlin is probably correct. I think that this business has its origin elsewhere."

"All right," Fiona conceded. "All right. What does that leave us with?"

"A mystery," he said. "But hardly, I think, an imminent threat."

A faint firefly of an idea flitted through my mind. It could easily be dead wrong, though that was not the reason I decided against sharing it. It led into an area of thought I could not explore in an instant, and I don't like giving away pieces of things like that.

Fiona was glaring at me now, but I maintained a bland expression. Abruptly then, seeing that her cause was fruitless, she decided to change the subject:

"You said that you left Luke under somewhat unusual circumstances. Just where is he now?"

The last thing I wanted to do was to get her really mad

at me. But I couldn't see turning her loose on Luke in his present condition. For all I knew, she might actually be up to killing him, just as a form of life insurance. And I did not want Luke dead. I'd a feeling he might be undergoing something of a change of attitude, and I wanted to give him every break I could. We still owed each other a few, even though it was hard keeping score; and there is something to be said for old times' sake. Considering what I'd judged his condition to be when I'd left him, it was going to be a while before he was in decent shape again. And then I had a number of things I wanted to talk to him about.

"Sorry," I said. "He's my province at the moment."

"I believe I have some interest in the matter," she replied levelly.

"Of course," I said, "but I feel that mine is greater and that we may get in each other's ways."

"I can judge these things for myself," she said.

"Okay," I told her. "He's on an acid trip. Any information you'd get out of him might be colorful, but it would also be highly disappointing."

"How did this happen?" she asked.

"A wizard named Mask apparently slipped him some chemicals when he had him prisoner."

"Where was this? I've never heard of Mask."

"A place called the Keep of the Four Worlds," I told her.

"It's been a long time since I heard the Keep mentioned," she said. "A sorcerer named Sharu Garrul used to hold it."

"He's a coatrack now," I stated.

"What?"

"Long story, but Mask has the place these days."

She stared at me, and I could tell she was just realizing that there was a lot she didn't know in the way of recent developments. I'd judge she was deciding which of several obvious questions to ask next when I decided to beat her to the punch while she was still off-balance.

"So how's Bleys?" I asked.

"He's much improved. I treated him myself and he's recovering quickly."

I was about to ask her where he was, which I knew she would refuse to answer, and hopefully we would both smile when she saw what I was driving at: no address for Bleys, no address for Luke; we keep our secrets and stay friends.

"Hello!" I heard Mandor say, and we both turned in the direction he was facing—back out through the notch.

The dark tornado-form had collapsed to half its former size, and even as we watched, it continued to diminish. It fell steadily in upon itself, shrinking and shrinking, and in about a half minute it was gone, completely.

I could not suppress a smile, but Fiona did not even notice. She was looking at Mandor.

"Do you think it was because of what you did?" she asked him.

"I have no way of knowing," he replied, "but it may well be."

"But does it tell you anything?" she said.

"Perhaps whoever was responsible did not like having me tinker with his experiment."

"You really believe there's an intelligence behind it?"

"Yes."

"Someone from the Courts?"

"It seems more likely than someone from your end of the world."

"I suppose so . . . ," she agreed. "Have you any guesses as to the person's identity?"

He smiled.

"I understand," she said quickly. "Your business is your business. But a general threat is everybody's business. That's what I was really getting at."

"True," he acknowledged. "This is why I propose investigating it. I'm at loose ends at the moment. It might be amusing."

"It is awkward asking you to communicate your

findings to me," she said, "when I do not know what interests might be involved."

"I appreciate your position," he replied, "but to the best of my knowledge the treaty provisions still hold and no one in the Courts is promoting any special designs against Amber. In fact. . . . If you like, we might pursue the matter together, at least part of the way."

"I've got the time," she said.

"I don't," I injected quickly. "I've some pressing business to attend to."

Mandor shifted his attention to me.

"About my offer . . . ," he said.

"I can't," I told him.

"Very well. Our conversation is not concluded, however. I'll be in touch later."

"Okay."

Fiona looked my way then, also.

"You will keep me posted on Luke's recovery, and his intentions," she stated.

"Of course."

"Good day, then."

Mandor gave me a small half-salute and I returned it. I began walking then, and as soon as I was out of sight I began shifting.

I found my way to a rocky slope, where I halted and withdrew my Trump for Amber. I raised it, focused my awareness, and transported myself as soon as I felt my way through. I was hoping the main hall would be empty, but at this point I didn't really care that much.

I came through near Jasra, who was holding an extra cloak over her outstretched left arm. I ducked out the doorway to my left into an empty corridor and made my way to the back stair. Several times I heard voices and I detoured to avoid the speakers. I was able to make it to my rooms without being discovered.

The only rest I had had in what seemed an age and a half had been a fifteen-minute nap before Luke's spaced-out sorcerous faculty had caused him to summon me to the Looking Glass Bar via a hallucinatory Trump. When? For all I knew, it could have been yesterday—which had been a very full day before that incident.

I barred the door and staggered to the bed, flinging myself down upon it without even removing my boots. Sure, there were all sorts of things I should be doing, but I was in no condition for any of them. I'd returned home because I still felt safest in Amber, despite the fact that Luke had reached me here once.

Someone with a high-powered subconscious might have had a brilliantly revelatory dream following as much crap as I'd been through recently, and then have awakened with a wonderful series of insights and answers detailing appropriate courses of action. I didn't. I woke once, in a small panic, not knowing where I was. But I opened my eyes and satisfied myself on that count, then went back to sleep. Later—much later, it seemed—I returned by degrees, like some piece of flotsam being pushed higher and higher onto a beach by wave following wave, until finally I was there. I saw no reason for going any further until I realized that my feet hurt. Then I sat up and pulled my boots off, which might have been one of the six greatest pleasures in my life. I removed my socks in a hurry then and threw them into the corner of the room. Why doesn't anyone else in my line of work seem to get sore feet? I filled the basin and soaked them for a time, then resolved to go barefoot for the next few hours.

Finally I rose, stripped, cleaned up, and put on a pair of Levi's and a purple flannel shirt of which I am fond. The hell with swords, daggers, and cloaks for a time. I opened the shutters and looked outside. It was dark. Because of clouds, I couldn't even guess from the stars whether it might be early evening, late night, or almost morning.

It was very quiet in the hall, and there were no sounds as I made my way down the back stair. The kitchen was deserted also, the big fires banked and smoldering low. I didn't want to stir things up beyond hanging a pot of water to warm for tea while I located some bread and fruit preserves. I turned up a jug of something like grapefruit juice, too, in one of the walk-in ice boxes.

As I sat warming my feet and working my way through the loaf, I began to feel uneasy. I was sipping my tea before I realized what it was. There seemed a great necessity that I be doing something, yet I had no idea what. Now I had something of a breather, and it felt strange. So I decided to start thinking again.

By the time I'd finished eating, I had a few small plans. The first thing I did was to make my way to the main hall, where I removed all of the hats and cloaks from Jasra and swept her off her feet. Later, as I was bearing her stiff form along the upstairs hallway in the direction of my room, a door opened partway and a bleary-eyed Droppa watched me go by.

"Hey, I'll take two!" he called after me.

"Reminds me of my first wife," he added then, and closed the door.

Once I had her installed in my quarters, I drew up a chair and seated myself before her. Garishly clad as part of a savage joke, her hard sort of beauty was not really diminished. She had placed me in extreme peril on one occasion, and I had no desire to free her at a time like this for a possible repeat performance. But the spell that held her claimed my attention for more than one reason, and I wanted to understand it fully.

Carefully then, I began exploring the construct which held her. It was not overcomplicated, but I could see that tracing all of its byways was going to take a while. All right. I wasn't about to stop now. I pushed on ahead into the spell, taking mental notes as I went.

I was busy for hours. After I had solved the spell, I decided to hang some more of my own, times being what they were. The castle came awake about me as I worked. I labored steadily as the day progressed, until everything was in place and I was satisfied with my work. I was also famished.

I moved Jasra off into a corner, pulled on my boots, departed my quarters, and headed for the stair. In that it seemed about lunchtime I checked out the several dining rooms in which the family generally ate. But all of them were deserted and none of them were set up for a meal yet to come. Nor did any of them show signs of a meal having recently been dispatched.

I suppose it was possible my time sense was still skewed and I was much too late or too early, but it did seem that it had been daylight long enough to bring me into the vicinity of the proper hour. Nobody, however, seemed to be eating, so something had to be wrong with this assumption. . . .

Then I heard it—the faint click of cutlery upon plate. I headed in the apparent direction of the sound. Obviously, the meal was taking place in a less frequented setting than usual. I turned right, then left. Yes, they had decided to set up in a drawing room. No matter.

I entered the room, where Llewella was seated with Random's wife, Vialle, on the red divan, dinner laid on a low table before them. Michael, who worked in the kitchen, stood nearby behind a cart loaded with dishes. I cleared my throat.

"Merlin," Vialle announced with a sensitivity that always gives me a small chill—she being completely blind. "How pleasant!"

"Hello," Llewella said. "Come and join us. We're anxious to hear what you've been doing."

I drew a chair up to the far side of the table and seated myself. Michael came over and laid a fresh setting before me. I thought about it quickly. Anything Vialle heard would doubtless get back to Random. So I gave them a somewhat edited version of recent events—leaving out all references to Mandor, Fiona, and anything having to do with the Courts. It made for a considerably shorter story and let me get to my food sooner.

"Everybody's been so busy lately," Llewella remarked when I'd finished talking. "It almost makes me feel guilty."

I studied the delicate green of her more-than-olive complexion, her full lips, her large catlike eyes.

"But not quite," she added.

"Where are they all, anyway?" I asked.

"Gérard," she said, "is down seeing to harbor fortifications, and Julian is in command of the army, which has now been equipped with some firearms and is set to defend the approaches to Kolvir."

"You mean Dalt has something in the field already? Coming this way?"

She shook her head. "No, it was a precautionary measure," she replied, "because of that message from Luke. Dalt's force had not actually been sighted."

"Does anyone even know where he is?" I asked.

"Not yet," she answered, "but we're expecting some intelligence on that soon." She shrugged. Then, "Perhaps Julian already has it," she added.

"Why is Julian in command?" I asked between nibbles. "I'd have thought Benedict would take charge of something like this."

Llewella looked away, glancing at Vialle, who seemed to feel the shifting of focus.

"Benedict and a small force of his men have escorted Random to Kashfa," Vialle said, softly.

"Kashfa?" I said. "Why would he want to do that? In fact, Dalt usually hangs out around Kashfa. The area could be dangerous right now."

She smiled faintly.

"That is why he wanted Benedict and his guard for escort," she said. "They may even be the intelligence-gathering expedition themselves, though that's not their reason for going right now."

"I don't understand," I said, "why the trip should be necessary at all."

She took a sip of water.

"A sudden political upheaval," she replied. "Some general had taken over in the absence of the queen and the crown prince. The general was just assassinated recently, and Random has succeeded in obtaining agreement for placing his own candidate—an older nobleman— on the throne."

"How'd he do that?"

"Everyone with an interest in the matter was even more interested in seeing Kashfa admitted to the Golden Circle of privileged trade status."

"So Random bought them off to see his own man in charge," I observed. "Don't these Golden Circle treaties usually give us the right to move troops through a client kingdom's territory with very little in the way of preliminaries?"

"Yes," she said.

I suddenly recalled that tough-looking emissary of the Crown I'd met at Bloody Bill's, who had paid his tab in Kashfan currency. I decided I did not really want to know how close in point of time that was to the assassination that had made this recent arrangement possible. What struck me with more immediate force was the picture that now emerged: It looked as if Random had just blocked Jasra and Luke from recovering their usurped throne— which, to be fair, I guess Jasra had usurped herself, years ago. With all that usurping going on, the equities of the thing were more than a little hazy to me. But if Random's ethics were no better than those which had gone before, they were certainly no worse. It looked now, though, as if any attempt on the part of Luke to regain his mother's throne would be met by a monarch who possessed a defense alliance with Amber. I suddenly felt willing to bet that the terms of the defense provisions of the alliance included Amber's assistance in internal troubles as well as help against outside aggressors.

Fascinating. It sounded as if Random were going to an awful lot of trouble to isolate Luke from his power base and any semblance of legitimacy as a head of state. I

supposed the next step could be to get him outlawed as
a pretender and a dangerous revolutionary, and to put a
price on his head. Was Random overreacting? Luke didn't
seem all that dangerous now, especially with his mother
in our custody. On the other hand, I didn't really know
how far Random intended to go. Was he just foreclosing
all of the threatening options, or was he actually out to
get Luke? The latter possibility bothered me in that Luke
seemed on halfway good behavior at the moment and
possibly in the throes of reconsidering his position. I did
not want to see him needlessly thrown to the wolves as
a result of overkill on Random's part.

So, "I suppose this has a lot to do with Luke," I said
to Vialle.

She was silent for a moment, then replied, "It was Dalt
that he seemed concerned about."

I shrugged mentally. It seemed that it would come
down to the same thing in Random's mind, since he
would see Dalt as the military force Luke would turn to
to recover the throne. So I said, "Oh," and went on
eating.

There were no new facts to be had beyond this, and
nothing to clarify Random's thinking any further, so we
lapsed into small talk while I considered my position once
again. It still came down to a feeling that urgent action
was necessary and uncertainty as to what form it should
take. My course was determined in an unexpected fashion
sometime during dessert.

A courtier named Randel—tall, thin, dark, and generally smiling—came into the room. I knew something was
up because he was not smiling and he was moving faster
than usual. He swept us with his gaze, fixed upon Vialle,
advanced quickly and cleared his throat.

"M'lady Majesty . . . ?" he began.

Vialle turned her head slightly in his direction.

"Yes, Randel?" she said. "What is it?"

"The delegation from Begma has just arrived," he
answered, "and I find myself without instructions as to

the nature of their welcome and any special arrangements that would be suitable."

"Oh dear!" Vialle said, laying aside her fork. "They weren't due until the day after tomorrow, when Random will be back. He's the one they'll be wanting to complain to. What have you done with them?"

"I seated them in the Yellow Room," he replied, "and told them I would go and announce their arrival."

She nodded.

"How many of them are there?"

"The prime minister, Orkuz," he said, "his secretary, Nayda—who is also his daughter—and another daughter, Coral. There are also four servants—two men and two women."

"Go and inform the household staff, and be sure that appropriate quarters are made ready for them," she directed, "and alert the kitchen. They may not have had lunch."

"Very good, Your Highness," he said, beginning to back away.

". . . Then report to me in the Yellow Room, to let me know it's been done," she continued, "and I'll give you additional instructions at that time."

"Consider it done," he replied, and he hurried off.

"Merlin, Llewella," Vialle said, beginning to rise, "come help me entertain them while arrangements are being made."

I gulped my last bite of dessert and got to my feet. I did not really feel like talking to a diplomat and his party, but I was handy and it was one of life's little duties.

"Uh. . . . What are they here for, anyway?" I asked.

"Some sort of protest over what we've been doing in Kashfa," she replied. "They've never been friendly with Kashfa, but I'm not sure now whether they're here to protest Kashfa's possible admission to the Golden Circle or whether they're upset about our interfering in Kashfa's domestic affairs. It could be they're afraid they'll lose business with such a close neighbor suddenly enjoying the samc preferred trade status they have. Or it may be they had different plans for Kashfa's throne and we just foreclosed them. Maybe both. Whatever. . . . We can't tell them anything we don't know."

"I just wanted to know what subjects to avoid," I said.

"All of the above," she answered.

"I was wondering the same thing myself," Llewella said. "I was also wondering, though, whether they might have any useful information on Dalt. Their intelligence service must keep a close eye on doings in and about Kashfa."

"Don't pursue that topic," Vialle said, moving toward the door. "If they let something slip or want to give something away, fine. Bring it home. But don't show them you'd like to know."

Vialle took my arm and I guided her out, heading toward the Yellow Room. Llewella produced a small mirror from somewhere and inspected her features. Obviously pleased, she put it away, then remarked, "Lucky you showed up, Merlin. An extra smiling face is always useful at times like this."

"Why don't I feel lucky?" I said.

We made our way to the room where the prime minister and his daughters waited. Their servants had already retired to the kitchen for refreshments. The official party was still hungry, which says something about protocol, especially since it seemed to take a long while before some trays of provender could be attractively assembled. Orkuz was of medium stature and stocky, his black hair tastefully streaked, the lines on his broad face seeming to indicate that he did a lot more frowning than smiling—a practice in which he indulged most of the while that afternoon. Nayda's was a more pleasingly sculpted version of his face, and though she showed the same tendency toward corpulence, it was held firmly in check at an attractive level of roundedness. Also, she smiled a lot and she had pretty teeth. Coral, on the other hand, was taller than either her father or sister, slender, her hair a reddish brown. When she smiled it seemed less official. Also, there was something vaguely familiar about her. I wondered whether I had met her at some boring reception years before. If I had, though, I felt I might have remembered.

After we had been introduced and wine had been poured, Orkuz made a brief comment to Vialle about "recent distressing news" concerning Kashfa. Llewella and I quickly moved to her side for moral support, but she simply said that such matters would have to be dealt with fully upon Random's return, and that for the moment she wished merely to see to their comfort. He was completely agreeable to this, even to the point of smiling. I had the impression he just wanted the purpose of his visit on the record immediately. Llewella quickly turned the conversation to the matter of his journey, and he graciously allowed the subject to be changed. Politicians are wonderfully programmed.

I learned later that the Begman ambassador wasn't even aware of his arrival, which would seem to indicate that Orkuz had come so quickly he had preceded any notification to their embassy. And he hadn't even bothered dropping in there, but had come straight to the palace and had a message sent over. I learned this a little later, when he asked to have the message delivered. Feeling somewhat supernumerary to Llewella's and Vialle's graceful cascades of neutral talk, I dropped back a pace to plan my escape. I was not at all interested in whatever game was being set up.

Coral backed off also and sighed. Then she glanced at me and smiled, surveyed the room quickly and came closer.

"I've always wanted to visit Amber," she said then.

"Is it the way you imagined it?" I asked.

"Oh, yes. So far. Of course, I haven't seen that much of it yet. . . ."

I nodded, and we withdrew a little farther from the others.

"Have I met you somewhere before?" I asked.

"I don't think so," she said. "I haven't traveled that much, and I don't believe you've been out our way. Have you?"

"No, though I've grown curious about it recently."

"I do know something of your background, though," she went on, "just from general gossip. I know you're from the Courts of Chaos, and I know you went to school on that Shadow world you Amberites seem to visit so frequently. I've often wondered what it was like."

I took the bait and I began telling her about school and my job, about a few places I'd visited and things I'd enjoyed doing. We made our way to a sofa across the room as I spoke, and we got more comfortable. Orkuz, Nayda, Llewella, and Vialle didn't seem to miss us, and if I had to be here I found talking with Coral more enjoyable than listening to them. Not to monopolize things, though, I asked her about herself.

She began telling me of a girlhood spent in and around Begma, of her fondness for the outdoors—of horses and of boating on the many lakes and rivers in that region—of books she had read, and of relatively innocent dabblings in magic. A member of the household staff came in just as she was getting around to a description of some interesting rites performed by members of the local farming community to insure the fertility of the crops, and she approached Vialle and told her something. Several more staff members were in view outside the doorway. Vialle then said something to Orkuz and Nayda, who nodded and moved toward the entrance. Llewella departed the group and came our way.

"Coral," she said, "your suite is ready. One of the staff will show you where it is. Perhaps you'd like to freshen up or rest after your journey."

We got to our feet.

"I'm not really tired," Coral said, looking at me rather than Llewella, a hint of a smile at the corners of her mouth.

What the hell. I suddenly realized I had been enjoying her company, so, "If you'd care to change into something simpler," I said, "I'll be glad to show you a bit of the town. Or the palace."

It became a full smile worth seeing.

"I'd much rather do that," she said.

"Then I'll meet you back here in about half an hour," I told her.

I saw her out, and accompanied her and the others as far as the foot of the big stairway. In that I still had on my Levi's and purple shirt, I wondered whether I should change into something more in keeping with local fashion. The hell with it, I decided then. We were just going to be knocking around. I'd simply add my swordbelt and weapons, a cloak, and my best boots. Might trim my beard, though, since I had a little time. And maybe a quick manicure. . . .

"Uh, Merlin. . . ."

It was Llewella, her hand on my elbow, steering me toward an alcove. I allowed myself to be steered.

Then, "Yes?" I said. "What's up?"

"Hm . . . ," she said. "Kind of cute, isn't she?"

"I suppose so," I replied.

"You got the hots for her?"

"Jeez, Llewella! I don't know. I just met the lady."

". . . And made a date with her."

"Come on! I deserve a break today. I enjoyed talking with her. I'd like to show her around a bit. I think we'd have a good time. What's wrong with that?"

"Nothing," she answered, "so long as you keep things in perspective."

"What perspective did you have in mind?"

"It strikes me as faintly curious," she said, "that Orkuz brought along his two good-looking daughters."

"Nayda *is* his secretary," I said, "and Coral's wanted to see the place for some time."

"Uh-huh, and it would be a very good thing for Begma

if one of them just happened to latch onto a member of the family.''

"Llewella, you're too damned suspicious," I said.

"It comes of having lived a long time."

"Well, I hope to live a long time myself, and I hope it doesn't make me look for an ulterior motive in every human act."

She smiled. "Of course. Forget I said anything," she told me, knowing I wouldn't. "Have a good time."

I growled politely and headed for my room.

CHAPTER 4

And so, in the midst of all manner of threats, intrigues, menaces, and mysteries, I decided to call a holiday and stroll about town with a pretty lady. Of all possible choices I might have made, it was certainly the most attractive. Whoever the enemy, whatever the power I faced, the ball was now in its court. I had no desire to hunt for Jurt, duel with Mask, or follow Luke about until he came down and told me whether or not he still wanted the family's scalps. Dalt was not my problem, Vinta was gone, Ghostwheel was silent, and the matter of my father's Pattern could await my leisure. The sun was shining and the breeze was gentle, though these could change quickly at this season. It was a shame to waste what could well be the year's last good day on anything less than enjoyment. I hummed as I repaired myself, and I headed downstairs early for our meeting.

Coral had moved more quickly than I'd guessed, however, and was waiting for me. I approved of her sensible dark green breeches, heavy coppery shirt, and warm brown cloak. Her boots looked fine for walking, and she had on a dark hat that covered most of her hair. There were gloves and a dagger at her belt.

"All ready," she said when she saw me.

"Great," I replied, smiling, and I led her out into the hallway.

She started to turn in the direction of the main

doorway, but I led her off to the right, then later to the left.

"Less conspicuous to use one of the side doors," I said.

"You people are certainly secretive," she said.

"Habit," I replied. "The less that outsiders know of your business the better."

"What outsiders? What are you afraid of?"

"Just now? A great number of things. But I don't really want to spend a nice day like this making lists."

She shook her head in what I took to be a mixture of awe and disgust.

"It's true what they say then?" she asked. "That your affairs are so complex you all carry scorecards?"

"Haven't had time for any affairs recently," I told her, "or even a simple score." Then, "Sorry," I added, when I saw her blush. "Life *has* been a bit complicated for me lately."

"Oh," she said, glancing at me, clearly asking for elaboration.

"Some other time," I said, forcing a laugh, flipping my cloak, and greeting a guard.

She nodded and, diplomatically, changed the subject:

"I guess I came at the wrong time of year to see your famous gardens."

"Yeah, they've pretty much had it for the season," I said, "except for Benedict's Japanese garden which is kind of far out back. Perhaps we can go and have a cup of tea there one day, but I thought we'd go into town now."

"Sounds fine," she agreed.

I told the postern guard to tell Henden, Amber's steward, that we were heading into town and weren't sure when we'd be back. He said that he would as soon as he got off duty, which would be pretty soon. My experience at Bloody Bill's had taught me the lesson of leaving such messages—not that I thought we were in any danger, or that Llewella's knowing wouldn't be sufficient.

Leaves crunched beneath our feet as we took one of the walks toward a side gate. With only a few strands of cirrus high overhead, the sun shone brightly. To the west, a flock of dark birds flapped its way toward the ocean, south.

"It's already snowed back home," she told me. "You're lucky."

"There's a warm current that gives us a break," I said, remembering something Gérard had once told me. "It moderates the climate considerably, compared to other places at equal latitude."

"You travel a lot?" she asked me.

"I've been traveling more than I care to," I said, "recently. I'd like to sit down and go to seed for about a year."

"Business or pleasure?" she asked me, as a guard let us out the gate and I quickly surveyed the environs for lurkers.

"Not pleasure," I answered as I took her elbow for a moment and steered her toward the way I had chosen.

When we reached civilized precincts, we followed the Main Concourse for a time. I pointed out a few landmarks and notable residences, including the Begman Embassy. She showed no inclination to visit the latter, though, saying she'd have to see her countrymen officially before she left, anyway. She did stop in a shop we found later, however, to buy a couple of blouses, having the bill sent to the embassy and the garments to the palace.

"My father promised me some shopping," she explained. "And I know he'll forget. When he hears about this, he'll know that I didn't."

We explored the streets of the various trades and stopped for a drink at a sidewalk cafe, watching pedestrians and horsemen pass. I had just turned toward her to relate an anecdote concerning one of the riders when I felt the beginning of a Trump contact. I waited for several seconds as the feeling grew stronger, but no identity took shape beyond the reaching. I felt Coral's hand upon my arm.

"What's the matter?" she asked.

I reached out with my mind, attempting to assist in the contact, but the other seemed to retreat as I did so. It was not the same as that lurking scrutiny when Mask had regarded me at Flora's place in San Francisco, though. Could it just be someone I knew trying to reach me and having trouble focusing? Injured, perhaps? Or—

"Luke?" I said. "Is that you?"

But there was no response and the feeling began to fade. Finally, it was gone.

"Are you all right?" Coral asked.

"Yeah, it's okay," I said. "I guess. Someone tried to reach me and then decided otherwise."

"Reach? Oh, you mean those Trumps you use?"

"Yes."

"But you said 'Luke' . . ." she mused. "None of your family is named—"

"You might know him as Rinaldo, Prince of Kashfa," I said.

She chuckled.

"Rinny? Sure I know him. He didn't like us to call him Rinny, though. . . ."

"You really *do* know him? Personally, I mean?"

"Yes," she replied, "though it's been a long time. Kashfa's pretty close to Begma. Sometimes we were on good terms, sometimes not so good. You know how it is. Politics. When I was little there were long spells when we were pretty friendly. There were lots of state visits, both ways. We kids would often get dumped together."

"What was he like in those days?"

"Oh, a big, gawky, red-haired boy. Liked to show off a lot—how strong he was, how fast he was. I remember how mad he got at me once because I beat him in a footrace."

"You beat Luke in a race?"

"Yes. I'm a very good runner."

"You must be."

"Anyway, he took Nayda and me sailing a few times, and on some long hikes. Where is he now, anyway?"

"Drinking with a Cheshire cat."

"What?"

"It's a long story."

"I'd like to hear it. I've been worried about him since the coup."

Mm. . . . I thought quickly about how to edit this so as not to tell the daughter of the Begman prime minister any state secrets, such as Luke's relationship to the House of Amber. . . . So, "I've known him for quite some time," I began. "He recently incurred the wrath of a sorcerer who drugged him and saw him banished to this peculiar bar. . . ."

I went on for a long while then, partly because I had to stop and summarize Lewis Carroll. I also had to promise her the loan of one of the Thari editions of *Alice* from the Amber library. When I finally finished, she was laughing.

"Why don't you bring him back?" she said then.

Ouch. I couldn't very well say that his shadow-shifting abilities would work against this until he came down. So, "It's part of the spell; it's working on his own sorcerous ability," I said. "He can't be moved till the drug wears off."

"How interesting," she observed. "Is Luke really a sorcerer himself?"

"Uh . . . yes," I said.

"How did he gain that ability? He showed no signs of it when I knew him."

"Sorcerers come by their skills in various ways," I explained. "But you know that," and I suddenly realized that she was smarter than that smiling, innocent expression indicated. I'd a strong feeling she was trying to steer this toward an acknowledgment of Pattern magic on Luke's part, which of course would say interesting things about his paternity. "And his mother, Jasra, is something of a sorceress herself."

"Really? I never knew that."

Damn! Coming and going. . . .

"Well, she'd learned it somewhere."

"What about his father?"

"I can't really say," I replied.

"Did you ever meet him?"

"Only in passing," I said.

A lie could make the matter seem really important if she had even a small idea as to the truth. So I did the only other thing I could think of. There was no one seated at the table behind her, and there was nothing beyond the table but a wall. I wasted one of my spells, with an out-of-sight gesture and a single mutter.

The table flipped over as it flew back and crashed against the wall. The noise was spectacular. There were loud exclamations from several other patrons, and I leaped to my feet.

"Is everyone all right?" I said, looking about as if for casualties.

"What happened?" she asked me.

"Freak gust of wind or something," I said. "Maybe we'd better be moving on."

"All right," she said, regarding the debris. "I'm not looking for trouble."

I tossed some coins onto our table, rose, and headed back outside, talking the while of anything I could think of to put some distance between us and the subject. This had the desired effect, because she did not attempt to retrieve the question.

Continuing our stroll, I headed us in the general direction of West Vine. When we reached it I decided to head downhill to the harbor, recalling her fondness for sailing. But she put her hand on my arm and halted me.

"Isn't there a big stairway up the face of Kolvir?" she asked. "I believe your father once tried to sneak troops up it and got caught and had to fight his way along."

I nodded. "Yes, that's true," I said. "Old thing. It goes way back. It's not used very much these days. But it's still in decent shape."

"I'd like to see it."

"All right."

I turned to the right and we headed back, uphill, toward the Main Concourse. A pair of knights wearing Llewella's livery passed us, headed in the other direction, saluting as they went by. I could not help but wonder whether they were on a legitimate errand or were following some standing order to keep an eye on my movements. The thought must have passed through Coral's mind, also, because she quirked an eyebrow at me. I shrugged and kept going. When I glanced back a bit later, they were nowhere to be seen.

We passed people in the garb of a dozen regions as we strolled, and the air was filled with the smells of cooking from open stalls, to satisfy a multitude of tastes. At various points in our career up the hill, we stopped for meat pies, yogurts, sweets. The stimuli were too overpowering for any but the most sated to ignore.

I noticed the lithe way she moved about obstacles. It wasn't just gracefulness. It was more a state of being—preparedness, I guess. Several times I noticed her glancing back in the direction from which we had come. I looked myself, but there was nothing unusual to see. Once, when a man stepped suddenly from a doorway we were approaching, I saw her hand flash toward the dagger at her belt, then drop away.

"There is so much activity, so much going on here . . . ," she commented after a time.

"True. Begma is less busy, I take it?"

"Considerably."

"Is it a pretty safe place to stroll about?"

"Oh, yes."

"Do the women as well as the men take military training there?"

"Not ordinarily. Why?"

"Just curious."

"I've had some training in armed and unarmed combat, though," she said.

"Why was that?" I asked.

"My father suggested it. Said it could come in handy for a relative of someone in his position. I thought he might be right. I think he really wanted a son."

"Did your sister do it, too?"

"No, she wasn't interested."

"You planning on a diplomatic career?"

"No. You're talking to the wrong sister."

"A wealthy husband?"

"Probably stodgy and boring."

"What, then?"

"Maybe I'll tell you later."

"All right. I'll ask if you don't."

We made our way southward along the Concourse, and the breezes picked up as we neared Land's End. It was a winter ocean that came into view across the distance, slate-gray and white-capped. Many birds wheeled far out over the waves, and one very sinuous dragon.

We passed through the Great Arch and came at last to the landing and looked downward. It was a vertiginous prospect, out across a brief, broad stair—the steep drop to the tan-and-black beach far below. I regarded the ripples in the sand left by the retreating tide, wrinkles in an old man's brow. The breezes were stronger here, and the damp, salty smell, which had been increasing as we approached, seasoned the air to a new level of intensity. Coral drew back for a moment, then advanced again.

"It looks a little more dangerous than I'd thought," she said, after a time. "Probably seems less so once you're on it."

"I don't know," I replied.

"You've never climbed it?"

"Nope," I said. "Never had any reason to."

"I'd think you'd have wanted to, after your father's doomed battle along it."

I shrugged. "I get sentimental in different ways."

She smiled. "Let's climb down to the beach. Please."

"Sure," I said, and we moved forward and started.

The broad stair took us down for perhaps thirty feet, then terminated abruptly where a much narrower version turned off to the side. At least the steps weren't damp and slippery. Somewhere far below, I could see where the stair widened again, permitting a pair of people to go abreast. For now, though, we moved single file, and I was irritated that Coral had somehow gotten ahead of me.

"If you'll scrunch over, I'll go past," I told her.

"Why?" she asked.

"So I can be ahead of you in case you slip."

"That's all right," she replied. "I won't."

I decided it wasn't worth arguing and let her lead.

The landings where the stairway switched back were haphazard affairs, hacked wherever the contours of the rock permitted such a turning. Consequently, some descending stretches were longer than others and our route wandered all over the face of the mountain. The winds were much stronger now than they were above, and we found ourselves staying as close to the mountain's side as its contours permitted. Had there been no wind, we probably would have done the same. The absence of any sort of guard railing made us shy back from the edge. There were places where the mountain's wall overhung us for a cavelike effect; other places, we followed a bellying of the rock and felt very exposed. My cloak blew up across my face several times and I cursed, recalling that natives seldom visit historical spots in their own neighborhoods. I began to appreciate their wisdom. Coral was hurrying on ahead, and I increased my pace to catch up with her. Beyond her, I could see that there was a landing which signaled the first turning of the way. I was hoping she'd halt there and tell me she'd reconsidered the necessity for this expedition. But she didn't. She turned and kept right on going. The wind stole my sigh and bore it to some storybook cave reserved for the plaints of the imposed-upon.

Still, I couldn't help but look down upon occasion; and whenever I did I thought of my father fighting his way up along these steps. It was not something I'd care to try—at least, not until I'd exhausted all of the more sneaky alternatives. I began to wonder how far we were below the level of the palace itself. . . .

When we finally came to the landing from which the stairway widened, I hurried to catch up with Coral so that we could walk abreast. In my haste, I snagged my heel and stumbled as I rounded the turn. It was no big deal. I was able to reach out and stabilize myself against the cliff's face as I jolted forward and swayed. I was amazed, though, at Coral's perception of my altered gait just on the basis of its sound, and by her reaction to it. She cast herself backward suddenly and twisted her body to the side. Her hands came in contact with my arm as she did this, and she thrust me to the side, against the rock.

"All right!" I said, from rapidly emptying lungs. "I'm okay."

She rose and dusted herself off as I recovered.

"I heard—" she began.

"I gather. But I just caught my heel. That's all."

"I couldn't tell."

"Everything's fine. Thanks."

We started down the stair side by side, but something was changed. I now harbored a suspicion I did not like but could not dispel. Not yet, anyway. What I had in mind was too dangerous, if I should prove correct.

So instead, "The rain in Spain stays mainly in the plain," I said.

"What?" she asked. "I didn't understand. . . ."

"I said, 'It's a fine day to be walking with a pretty lady.' "

She actually blushed.

Then, "What language did you say it in . . . the first time?"

"English," I replied.

"I've never studied it. I told you that when we were talking about *Alice*."

"I know. Just being whimsical," I answered.

The beach, nearer now, was tiger-striped and shiny in places. A froth of foam retreated along its slopes while birds cried and dipped to examine the waves' leavings. Sails bobbed in the offing, and a small curtain of rain rippled in the southeast, far out at sea. The winds had ceased their noise-making, though they still came upon us with cloak-wrapping force.

We continued in silence until we had reached the bottom. We stepped away then, moving a few paces onto the sand.

"The harbor's in that direction," I said, gesturing to my right, westward, "and there's a church off that way," I added, indicating the dark building where Caine's service had been held and where seamen sometimes came to pray for safe voyages.

She looked in both directions and also glanced behind us and upward.

"More people headed down," she remarked.

I looked back up and saw three figures near the top of the stairway, but they were standing still, as if they'd only come down a short distance to try the view. None of them wore Llewella's colors. . . .

"Fellow sightseers," I said.

She watched them a moment longer, then looked away.

"Aren't there caves along here somewhere?" she asked.

I nodded to my right.

"That way," I answered. "There's a whole series. People get lost in them periodically. Some are pretty colorful. Others just wander through darkness. A few are simply shallow openings."

"I'd like to see them," she said.

"Sure, easily done. Let's go."

I began walking. The people on the stair had not

moved. They still appeared to be looking out to sea. I
doubted they were smugglers. It doesn't seem like a
daytime occupation for a place where anyone might
wander by. Still, I was pleased that my faculty for suspicion was growing. It seemed appropriate in light of recent
events. The object of my greatest suspicion, of course,
was walking beside me, turning driftwood with the toe of
her boot, scuffing bright pebbles, laughing—but there was
nothing I was ready to do about it at the moment.
Soon. . . .

She took my arm suddenly.

"Thanks for bringing me," she said. "I'm enjoying
this."

"Oh, I am, too. Glad we came. You're welcome."

This made me feel slightly guilty, but if my guess were
wrong no harm would be done.

"I think I would enjoy living in Amber," she remarked
as we went along.

"Me, too," I replied. "I've never really done it for
any great length of time."

"Oh?"

"I guess I didn't really explain how long I'd spent on
the shadow Earth where I went to school, where I had
that job I was telling you about . . . ," I began, and
suddenly I was pouring out more autobiography to her—
a thing I don't usually do. I wasn't certain why I was
telling it at first, and then I realized that I just wanted
someone to talk to. Even if my strange suspicion was
correct, it didn't matter. A friendly-seeming listener made
me feel better than I had in a long while. And before I
realized it, I was telling her about my father—how this
man I barely knew had rushed through a massive story of
his struggles, his dilemmas, his decisions, as if he were
trying to justify himself to me, as if that were the only
opportunity he might have to do it, and how I had
listened, wondering what he was editing, what he had
forgotten, what he might be glossing over or dressing up,
what his feelings were toward me. . . .

"Those are some of the caves," I told her, as they interrupted my now embarrassing indulgence in memory. She started to say something about my monologue, but I simply continued, "I've only seen them once."

She caught my mood and simply said, "I'd like to go inside one."

I nodded. They seemed a good place for what I had in mind.

I chose the third one. Its mouth was larger than the first two, and I could see back into it for a good distance.

"Let's try that one. It looks well lighted," I explained.

We walked into a shadow-hung chill. The damp sand followed us for a while, thinning only slowly to be replaced by a gritty stone floor. The roof dipped and rose several times. A turn to the left joined us with the passage of another opening, for looking back along it I could see more light. The other direction led more deeply into the mountain. We could still feel the echoing pulse of the sea from where we stood.

"These caves could lead back really far," she observed.

"They do," I replied. "They twist and cross and wind. I wouldn't want to go too far without a map and a light. They've never been fully charted, that I know of."

She looked about, studying areas of blackness within the darkness where side tunnels debouched into our own.

"How far back do you think they go?" she inquired.

"I just don't know."

"Under the palace?"

"Probably," I said, remembering the series of side tunnels I'd passed on my way to the Pattern. "It seems possible they cut into the big caves below it—somewhere."

"What's it like down there?"

"Under the palace? Just dark and big. Ancient. . . ."

"I'd like to see it."

"Whatever for?"

"The Pattern's down there. It must be pretty colorful."

"Oh, it is—all bright and swirly. Rather intimidating, though."

"How can you say that when you've walked it?"

"Walking it and liking it are two different things."

"I'd just thought that if it were in you to walk it, you'd feel some affinity, some deep resonant kinship with it."

I laughed, and the sounds echoed about us.

"Oh, while I was walking it I knew it was in me to do it," I said. "I didn't feel it beforehand, though. I was just scared then. And I never liked it."

"Strange."

"Not really. It's like the sea or the night sky. It's big and it's powerful and it's beautiful and it's there. It's a natural force and you make of it what you will."

She looked back along the passageway leading inward.

"I'd like to see it," she said.

"I wouldn't try to find my way to it from here," I told her. "Why do you want to see it, anyhow?"

"Just to see how I'd respond to something like that."

"*You're* strange," I said.

"Will you take me when we go back? Will you show it to me?"

This was not going at all the way I'd thought it would. If she were what I thought, I didn't understand the request. I was half-tempted to take her to it, to find out what she had in mind. However, I was operating under a system of priorities, and I'd a feeling she represented one concerning which I'd made myself a promise and some elaborate preparations.

"Perhaps," I mumbled.

"Please. I'd really like to see it."

She seemed sincere. But my guess felt near-perfect. Sufficient time had passed for that strange body-shifting spirit, which had dogged my trail in many forms, to have located a new host and then to have zeroed in on me again and be insinuating itself into my good graces once more. Coral was perfect for the role, her arrival appropriately timed, her concern for my physical welfare manifest, her reflexes fast. I'd have liked to keep her around for questioning, but I knew that she would simply lie to me in the absence of proof or an emergency situation. And I did not trust her. So I reviewed the spell I had prepared and hung on my way home from Arbor House, a spell I had designed to expel a possessing entity from its host. I hesitated a moment, though. My feelings toward her were ambivalent. Even if she were the entity, I might be willing to put up with her if I just knew her motive.

So, "What is it that you want?" I asked.

"Just to see it. Honestly," she answered.

"No, I mean that if you are what I think you really are, I'm asking the big question: Why?"

Frakir began to pulse upon my wrist.

Coral was silent for the space of an audible deep breath, then, "How could you tell?"

"You betrayed yourself in small ways discernible only to one who has recently become paranoid," I responded.

"Magic," she said. "Is that it?"

"It's about to be," I replied. "I could almost miss you, but I can't trust you."

I spoke the guide words to the spell, letting them draw my hands smoothly through the appropriate gestures.

There followed two horrible shrieks, and then a third. But they weren't hers. They came from around the corner in the passageway we had recently quitted.

"What—?" she began.

"—the hell!" I finished, and I rushed past her and rounded the corner, drawing my blade as I went.

Backlighted by the distant cavemouth I beheld three figures on the floor of the cave. Two of them were sprawled and unmoving. The third was seated and bent forward, cursing. I advanced slowly, the point of my weapon directed toward the seated one. His shadowy head turned in my direction, and he climbed to his feet, still bent forward. He clutched his left hand with his right, and he backed away until he came into contact with the wall.

He halted there, muttering something I could not quite hear. I continued my cautious advance, all of my senses alert. I could hear Coral moving at my back, then I glimpsed her accompanying me on my left when the passage widened. She had drawn her dagger, and she held it low and near to her hip. No time now to speculate as to what my spell might have done to her.

I halted as I came to the first of the two fallen forms. I prodded it with the toe of my boot, ready to strike instantly should it spring into an attack. Nothing. It felt limp, lifeless. I used my foot to turn it over, and the head rolled back in the direction of the cavemouth. In the light that then fell upon it I beheld a half-decayed human face. My nose had already been informing me that this state was no mere illusion. I advanced upon the other one and turned him, also. He, too, bore the appearance of a decomposing corpse. While the first one clutched a dagger in his right hand, the second was weaponless. Then I noted another dagger—on the floor, near the live man's feet. I raised my eyes to him. This made no sense whatsoever. I'd have judged the two figures upon the floor to have been dead for several days, at least, and I had no idea as to what the standing man had been up to.

"Uh. . . . Mind telling me what's going on?" I inquired.

"Damn you, Merlin!" he snarled, and I recognized the voice.

I moved in a slow arc, stepping over the fallen ones. Coral stayed near to my side, moving in a similar fashion. He turned his head to follow our progress, and when the light finally fell upon his face, I saw that Jurt was glaring at me out of his one good eye—a patch covered the other—and I saw, too, that about half of his hair was missing, the exposed scalp covered with welts or scars, his half-regrown ear-stub plainly visible. From this side I could also see that a bandana suitable for covering most of this damage had slipped down around his neck. Blood was dripping from his left hand, and I suddenly realized that his little finger was missing.

"What happened to you?" I asked.

"One of the zombies hit my hand with his dagger as he fell," he said, "when you expelled the spirits that animated them."

My spell—to evict a possessing spirit. . . . They had been within range of it. . . .

"Coral," I asked, "are you all right?"

"Yes," she replied. "But I don't understand. . . ."

"Later," I told her.

I did not ask him about his head, as I recalled my struggle with the one-eyed werewolf in the wood to the east of Amber—the beast whose head I had forced into the campfire. I had suspected for some time that it had been Jurt in a shape-shifted form, even before Mandor had offered sufficient information to confirm it.

"Jurt," I began, "I have been the occasion of many of your ills, but you must realize that you brought them on yourself. If you would not attack me, I would have no need to defend myself—"

There came a clicking, grinding sound. It took me several seconds to realize that it was a gnashing of teeth.

"My adoption by your father meant nothing to me," I said, "beyond the fact that he honored me by it. I was not even aware until recently that it had occurred."

"You lie!" he hissed. "You tricked him some way, to get ahead of us in the succession."

"You've got to be kidding," I said. "We're all so far down on the list that it doesn't matter."

"Not for the Crown, you fool! For the House! Our father isn't all that well!"

"I'm sorry to hear that," I said. "But I'd never even thought of it that way. And Mandor's ahead of all of us, anyhow."

"And now you're second."

"Not by choice. Come on! I'll never see the title. You know that!"

He drew himself upright, and when he moved I became aware of a faint prismatic nimbus that had been clinging to his outline.

"That isn't the real reason," I continued. "You've never liked me, but you're not after me because of the succession. You're hiding something now. It's got to be something else, for all this activity on your part. By the way, you did send the Fire Angel, didn't you?"

"It found you that fast?" he said. "I wasn't even sure I could count on that. I guess it was worth the price after all. But. . . . What happened?"

"It's dead."

"You're very lucky. Too lucky," he replied.

"What is it that you want, Jurt? I'd like to settle this once and for all."

"Me, too," he answered. "You betrayed someone I love, and only your death will set things right."

"Who are you talking about? I don't understand."

He grinned suddenly.

"You will," he said. "In the last moments of your life I'll let you know why."

"I may have a long wait, then," I answered. "You don't seem to be very good at this sort of thing. Why not just tell me now and save us both a lot of trouble?"

He laughed, and the prism effect increased, and it occurred to me in that instant what it was.

"Sooner than you think," he said, "for shortly I will be more powerful than anything you ever met."

"But no less clumsy," I suggested, both to him and to whomever held his Trump, watching me through it, ready to snatch him away in an instant. . . .

"That *is* you, Mask, isn't it?" I said. "Take him back. You don't have to send him again either and watch him screw up. I'll promote you on my list of priorities and come calling soon, if you'll just give me an assurance that it's really you."

Jurt opened his mouth and said something, but I couldn't hear it because he faded fast and his words went

away with him. Something flew toward me as this
occurred; there was no need to parry it, but I couldn't
stop the reflex.

Along with two moldering corpses and Jurt's little
finger, a dozen or so roses lay scattered on the floor at
my feet, there at the rainbow's end.

CHAPTER 5

As we walked along the beach in the direction of the harbor, Coral finally spoke:

"Does that sort of thing happen around here very often?"

"You should come by on a bad day," I said.

"If you don't mind telling me, I'd like to hear what it was all about."

"I guess I owe you an explanation," I agreed, "because I wronged you back there, whether you know it or not."

"You're serious."

"Yep."

"Go on. I'm really curious."

"It's a long story . . . ," I began again.

She looked ahead to the harbor, then up to Kolvir's heights.

". . . A long walk, too," she said.

". . . And you're a daughter of the prime minister of a country with which we have somewhat touchy relations at the moment."

"What do you mean?"

"Some of the things that are happening may represent kind of sensitive information."

She put her hand on my shoulder and halted. She stared into my eyes.

"I can keep a secret," she told me. "After all, you know mine."

80

I congratulated myself on having finally learned my relatives' trick of controlling facial expression even when puzzled as all hell. She *had* said something back in the cave when I had addressed her as if she were the entity, something that sounded as if she believed I had discovered a secret concerning her.

So I gave her a wry smile and nodded.

"Just so," I said.

"You're not planning on ravaging our country or anything like that, are you?" she asked.

"To my knowledge, no. And I don't think it likely either."

"Well, then. You can only speak from your knowledge, can't you?"

"True," I agreed.

"So let's hear the story."

"All right."

As we walked along the strand and I spoke, to the accompaniment of the waves' deep notes, I could not help but remember again my father's long narrative. Was it a family trait, I wondered, to go autobiographical at a time of troubles if the right listener turned up? For I realized I was elaborating my telling beyond the bounds of necessity. And why should she be the right listener, anyhow?

When we reached the port district, I realized I was hungry, anyway, and I still had a lot of telling to do. In that it was still daylight and doubtless considerably safer than when I'd made my nighttime visit, I found my way over to Harbor Road—which was even dirtier in strong light—and, having learned that Coral was hungry, too, I took us on around to the rear of the cove, pausing for a few minutes to watch a many-masted vessel with golden sails round the sea wall and head in. Then we followed the curving way to the western shore, and I was able to locate Seabreeze Lane without any trouble. It was still early enough that we passed a few sober sailors. At one point a heavy, black-bearded man with an interesting scar on his right cheek began to approach us, but a smaller man caught up with him first and whispered something in his ear. They both turned away.

"Hey," I said. "What did he want?"

"Nothin'," the smaller man said. "He don't want nothin'." He studied me for a moment and nodded. Then, "I saw you here the other night," he added.

"Oh," I said, as they continued to the next corner, turned it, and were gone.

"What was that all about?" Coral said.

"I didn't get to that part of the story yet."

But I remembered it vividly when we passed the place where it had occurred. No signs of that conflict remained.

I almost passed what had been Bloody Bill's, though, because a new sign hung above the door. It read "Bloody Andy's," in fresh green letters. The place was just the same inside, however, except for the man behind the counter, who was taller and thinner than the shaggy, crag-faced individual who had served me last time. His name, I learned, was Jak, and he was Andy's brother. He sold us a bottle of Bayle's Piss and put in our order for two fish dinners through the hole in the wall. My former table was vacant and we took it. I laid my sword belt on the chair to my right, with the blade partly drawn, as I had been taught etiquette required here.

"I like this place," she said. "It's . . . different."

"Uh . . . yes," I agreed, glancing at two passed-out drunks—one to the front of the establishment, one to the rear—and three shifty-eyed individuals conversing in low voices off in one corner. A few broken bottles and suspicious stains were upon the floor, and some not-too-subtle artwork of an amorous nature hung on the far wall. "The food's quite good," I added.

"I've never been in a restaurant like this," she continued, watching a black cat, who rolled in from a rear room, wrestling with an enormous rat.

"It has its devotees, but it's a well-kept secret among discriminating diners."

I continued my tale through a meal even better than the

one I remembered. When the door opened much later to admit a small man with a bad limp and a dirty bandage about his head I noticed that daylight was beginning to wane. I had just finished my story and it seemed a good time to be leaving.

I said as much, but she put her hand on mine.

"You know I'm not your entity," she said, "but if you need any kind of help I can give you, I'll do it."

"You're a good listener," I said. "Thanks. We'd better be going now."

We passed out of Death Alley without incident and made our way along Harbor Road over to Vine. The sun was getting ready to set as we headed upward, and the cobbles passed through a variety of bright earth tones and fire colors. Street and pedestrian traffic was light. Cooking smells drifted on the air; leaves rattled along the road; a small yellow dragon rode the air currents high overhead; curtains of rainbow light rippled high in the north beyond the palace. I kept waiting, expecting more questions from Coral than the few she had asked. They never came. If I'd just heard my story, I think I'd have a lot of questions, unless I were totally overpowered by it or somehow understood it thoroughly.

"When we get back to the palace . . . ?" she said then.

"Yes?"

". . . You *will* take me to see the Pattern, won't you?"

I laughed.

. . . Or unless something else were occupying my mind.

"Right away? First thing in the door?" I asked.

"Yes."

"Sure," I said.

Then, that off her mind, "Your story changes my picture of the world," she said, "and I wouldn't presume to advise you. . . ."

"But—" I continued.

". . . It seems that the Keep of the Four Worlds holds

the answers you want. Everything else may fall into place when you learn what's going on there. But I don't understand why you can't just do a card for it and trump in."

"Good question. There are parts of the Courts of Chaos to which no one can trump because they change constantly and cannot be represented in a permanent fashion. The same applies to the place where I situated Ghostwheel. Now, the terrain around the Keep fluctuates quite a bit, but I'm not positive that's the reason for the blockage. The place is a power center, and I think it possible that someone diverted some of that power into a shielding spell. A good enough magician might be able to drill through it with a Trump, but I've a feeling that the force required would probably set off some psychic alarm and destroy any element of surprise."

"What does the place look like, anyway?" she asked.

"Well . . . ," I began. "Here." I took my notebook and Scripto from my shirt pocket and sketched. "See, all of this area is volcanic." I scribbled in a few fumaroles and wisps of smoke. "And this part is Ice Age." More scribbles. "Ocean here, mountains here. . . ."

"Then it sounds as if your best bet is to use the Pattern again," she said, studying the drawing and shaking her head.

"Yes."

"Do you think you'll be doing it soon?"

"Possibly."

"How will you attack them?"

"I'm still working on that."

"If there's any sort of way that I can help you, I meant what I said."

"There isn't."

"Don't be so sure. I'm well trained. I'm resourceful. I even know a few spells."

"Thanks," I said. "But no."

"No discussion?"

"Nope."

"If you change your mind. . . ."

"I won't."

". . . Let me know."

We reached the Concourse, moved along it. The winds grew more blustery here and something cold touched my cheek. Then again. . . .

"Snow!" Coral announced, just as I realized that a few middle-sized flakes were drifting past us, vanishing immediately when they hit the ground.

"If your party had arrived at the proper time," I observed, "you might not have had your walk."

"Sometimes I'm lucky," she said.

It was snowing fairly hard by the time we reached the palace grounds. We used the postern gate again, pausing on the walkway to gaze back down over the light-dotted town, half-screened by falling flakes. I knew she kept looking longer than I did, because I turned to gaze at her. She appeared—happy, I guess—as if she were pasting the scene in a mental scrapbook. So I leaned over and kissed her cheek, because it seemed like a good idea.

"Oh," she said, turning to face me. "You surprised me."

"Good," I told her. "I hate to telegraph these things. Let's get the troops in out of the cold."

She smiled and took my arm.

Inside, the guard told me, "Llewella wants to know whether you two will be joining them all for dinner."

"When *is* dinner?" I asked him.

"In about an hour and a half, I believe."

I glanced at Coral, who shrugged.

"I guess so," I said.

"Front dining room, upstairs," he told me. "Shall I pass the word to my sergeant—he's due by soon—and have him deliver it? Or do you want to—"

"Yes," I said. "Do that."

"Care to wash up, change clothes . . . ?" I began, as we walked away.

"The Pattern," she said.

"It would involve a lot more stairs," I told her.

She turned toward me, her face tightening, but saw that I was smiling.

"This way," I said, leading her to the main hall and through it.

I didn't recognize the guard at the end of the brief corridor that led up to the stair. He knew who I was, though, glanced curiously at Coral, opened the door, found us a lantern, and lit it.

"I'm told there's a loose step," he remarked as he passed me the light.

"Which one is it?"

He shook his head.

"Prince Gérard's reported it several times," he said, "but no one else seems to notice it."

"Okay," I said. "Thanks."

This time Coral didn't object to my going first. Of the two, this was more intimidating than the stairway on the cliff face, mainly because you can't see bottom and after a few paces you can't see much of anything beyond the shell of light within which you move as you wind your way down. And there's a heavy sense of vastness all about you. I've never seen the place illuminated, but I gather that the impression is not incorrect. It's a very big cavern, and you go round and round and down in the middle of it, wondering when you'll reach the bottom.

After a time, Coral cleared her throat, then, "Could we stop for a minute?" she asked.

"Sure," I said, halting. "Out of breath?"

"No," she said. "How much farther?"

"I don't know," I replied. "It seems a different distance each time I come this way. If you want to go back and have dinner, we can see it tomorrow. You've had a busy day."

"No," she answered. "But I wouldn't mind your holding me for a minute."

It seemed an awkward place to get romantic, so I

cleverly deduced that there was another reason, said nothing, and obliged.

It took me a long while to realize that she was crying. She was very good at concealing it.

"What's the matter?" I finally asked.

"Nothing," she replied. "Nervous reaction, maybe. Primitive reflex. Darkness. Claustrophobia. Like that."

"Let's go back."

"No."

So we started down again.

About a half minute later I saw something white near the side of a lower step. I slowed. Then I realized that it was only a handkerchief. A little nearer, however, and I saw that it was held in place by a dagger. Also, there were markings upon it. I halted, reached out, flattened it, and read. "THIS ONE, DAMN IT! —GÉRARD," it said.

"Careful here," I said to Coral.

I prepared to step over it, but on an impulse I tested it lightly with one foot. No squeaks. I shifted more weight onto it. Nothing. It felt firm. I stood on it. The same. I shrugged.

"Careful, anyway," I said.

Nothing happened when she stepped on it either, and we kept going. A little later, I saw a flicker in the distance below. It was moving, and I guessed someone was doing a patrol. What for? I wondered. Were there prisoners to be tended and watched? Were certain cave mouths considered vulnerable points? And what about the business of locking the chamber of the Pattern and hanging the key on the wall near the door? Was there some possible danger from that quarter? How? Why? I realized that I ought to pursue these questions one of these days.

When we reached the bottom the guard was nowhere in sight, however. The table, the racks, and a few foot lockers—which constituted the guard station—were illuminated by a number of lanterns, but the guard was not at his post. Too bad. It would be interesting to ask

what the orders called for in the event of an emergency—
hopefully also specifying the possible natures of various
emergencies. For the first time, though, I noticed a rope
hanging down from the darkness into the dimness beside
a weapons rack. I drew upon it ever so gently and it
yielded, to be followed a moment later by a faint metallic
sound from somewhere high overhead. Interesting.
Obviously, this was the alarm.

"Which . . . way?" Coral asked.

"Oh, come on," I said, taking her hand, and I led her
off to the right.

I kept waiting for echoes as we moved, but none came.
Periodically, I raised the light. The darkness would recede
a bit then, but nothing came into view beyond an
additional area of floor.

Coral seemed to be slowing now, and I felt a certain
tension in her arm as she hung back. I plodded on and
she kept moving, however.

Finally, "It shouldn't be too much longer," I said, as
the echoes began, very faintly.

"Good," she replied, but she did not increase her pace.

At last the gray wall of the cavern came into view, and
far off to my left was the dark opening of the tunnel
mouth I sought. I changed course and headed toward it.
When we finally reached it and entered, I felt her flinch.

"If I'd known it would bother you this much—" I
began.

"I'm really all right," she answered, "and I do want
to see it. I just didn't realize that getting there would be
this . . . involved."

"Well, the worst of it is over. Soon now," I said.

We came to the first side passage to the left fairly
quickly and went on by. There was another shortly thereafter, and I slowed and extended the lantern toward it.

"Who knows?" I commented. "That could take you
through some strange route back to the beach."

"I'd rather not check it out."

We walked for some time before we passed the third

opening. I gave it a quick glance. There was a vein of some bright mineral partway back in it.

I speeded up and she kept pace, our footsteps ringing loudly now. We passed the fourth opening. The fifth. . . . From somewhere, it seemed I heard faint strains of music.

She glanced at me inquiringly when we neared the sixth passageway, but I just kept going. It was the seventh that I wanted, and when we finally came to it I turned, took a few paces, halted, and raised the lantern. We stood before a big metal-bound door.

I took the key down from the hook on the wall to my right, inserting it in the lock, turned it, withdrew it, and rehung it. Then I put my shoulder against the door and pushed hard. There followed a long moment of resistance, then slow movement accompanied shortly by a complaint from a tight hinge. Frakir tightened upon my wrist, but I kept pushing till the door was opened wide. Then I stood to the side and held it for Coral.

She moved a few steps past me into that strange chamber and halted. I stepped away and let the door swing shut, then came up beside her.

"So that's it," she remarked.

Roughly elliptical, the intricately wound oval form of the Pattern glowed blue-white within the floor. I set the lantern aside. It wasn't really necessary, the glow from the Pattern providing more than sufficient illumination. I stroked Frakir, calming her. A jet of sparks rose at the far end of the great design, subsided quickly, occurred again nearer to us. The chamber seemed filled with a half-familiar pulsing I had never consciously noted before. On an impulse—to satisfy a long-held point of curiosity—I summoned the Sign of the Logrus.

This was a mistake.

Immediately the image of the Logrus flared before me, sparks erupted along the entire length of the Pattern, and a high-pitched banshee wail rose from somewhere. Frakir went wild, my ears felt as if icicles had been driven into them, and the brightness of the writhing Sign hurt my eyes. I banished the Logrus in that instant, and the turmoil began to subside.

"What," she asked me, "was that?"

I tried to smile, didn't quite manage it.

"A little experiment I'd always meant to try," I told her.

"Did you learn anything from it?"

"Not to do it again, perhaps," I answered.

"Or at least not till the company's left," she said. "That hurt."

"Sorry."

She moved nearer to the edge of the Pattern, which had calmed itself again.

"Eerie," she observed. "Like a light in a dream. But it's gorgeous. And all of you have to walk it to come into your heritage?"

"Yes."

She moved slowly to the right, following its perimeter. I followed her as she strolled, her gaze roving across the bright expanse of arcs and turns, short straight lines, long sweeping curves.

"I assume it is difficult?"

"Yes. The trick is to keep pushing and not to stop trying even if you stop moving," I replied.

We walked on, to the right, circling slowly around to the rear. The design seemed to be within the floor rather than upon it, seen as through a layer of glass. But nowhere was the surface slippery.

We paused for a minute or so while she took its measure from a new angle.

"So how are you responding to it?" I finally asked.

"Esthetically," she said.

"Anything else?"

"Power," she said. "It seems to radiate something." She leaned forward and waved her hand above the nearest line. "It's almost a physical pressure," she added then.

We moved farther, passing along the back length of the

grand design. I could see across the Pattern, to the place where the lantern glowed on the floor near to the entranceway. Its light was negligible beside the greater illumination we regarded now.

Shortly, Coral halted again. She pointed.

"What is this single line, which seems to end right here?" she asked.

"It's not the end," I said. "It's the beginning. That is the place where one commences the walking of the Pattern."

She moved nearer, passing her hand above it also.

"Yes," she said after a moment. "I can feel that it starts here."

For how long we stood there, I am uncertain. Then she reached out, took hold of my hand and squeezed it.

"Thanks," she said, "for everything."

I was about to ask her why that had such a final sound about it, when she moved forward and set her foot upon the line.

"No!" I cried. "Stop!"

But it was too late. Her foot was already in place, brightness outlining the sole of her boot.

"Don't move!" I said. "Whatever you do, stay still!"

She did as I said, holding her position. I licked my lips, which suddenly seemed very dry.

"Now, try to raise the foot you placed upon the line and draw it back. Can you do it?"

"No," she replied.

I knelt beside her and studied it. Theoretically, once you'd set foot upon the Pattern there was no turning back. You had no choice but to continue and either make it through or be destroyed somewhere along the way. On the other hand, she should already be dead. Theoretically, again, anyone not of the blood of Amber shouldn't be able to set foot upon it and live. So much for theory.

"Hell of a time to ask," I said. "But why'd you do it?"

"You indicated to me back in the cave that my guess was correct. You said that you knew what I was."

I recalled what I'd said, but that was with reference to my guess at her being the body-shifting entity. What could she have taken it to mean that had to do with the Pattern? But even as I sought after a spell that might free her from the Pattern's hold, the obvious answer to things drifted into my mind.

"Your connection with the House . . . ?" I said softly.

"King Oberon supposedly had an affair with my mother before I was born," she said. "The timing would have been right. It was only a rumor, though. I couldn't get anyone to provide details. So I was never certain. But I dreamed of it being true. I wanted it to be true. I hoped to find some tunnel that would bring me to this place. I wanted to sneak in and walk the Pattern and have the shadows unfold before me. But I was afraid, too, because I knew that if I were wrong I would die. Then, when you said what you said, you answered my dream. But I did not stop being afraid. I am still afraid. Only now I'm afraid that I won't be strong enough to make it."

That sense of familiarity I had felt when I first met her. . . . I suddenly realized that it was a general family resemblance that had caused it. Her nose and brow reminded me a bit of Fiona, her chin and cheekbones something of Flora. Her hair and eyes and height and build were her own, though. But she certainly did not resemble her nominal father or sister.

I thought again of a faintly leering portrait of my grandfather which I had often studied, in an upstairs hallway, to the west. The lecherous old bastard really got around. Giving him his due, though, he was a very good-looking man. . . .

I sighed and rose to my feet. I laid a hand upon her shoulder.

"Listen, Coral," I said. "All of us were well briefed before we tried it. I am going to tell you about it before you take another step, and while I speak you may feel energy flowing from me into you. I want you to be as strong as possible. When you take your next step I do not want you to stop again until you have reached the middle. I may call out instructions to you as you move along, also. Do whatever I say immediately, without thinking about it.

"First I will tell you about the Veils, the places of resistance. . . ."

For how long I spoke, I do not know.

I watched as she approached the First Veil.

"Ignore the chill and the shocks," I said. "They can't hurt you. Don't let the sparks distract you. You're about to hit major resistance. Don't start breathing rapidly."

I watched her push her way through.

"Good," I said, as she came onto an easier stretch, deciding against telling her that the next Veil was far worse. "By the way, don't think that you're going crazy. Shortly, it will begin playing head games with you—"

"It already has," she responded. "What should I do?"

"It's probably mostly memories. Just let them flow, and keep your attention on the path."

She continued, and I talked her through the Second Veil. The sparks reached almost to her shoulders before she was out of it. I watched her struggle through arc after arc, then tricky curves and long, sweeping ones, turns, reversals. There were times when she moved quickly, times when she was slowed almost to a standstill. But she kept moving. She had the idea, and it seemed she had the will. I did not think that she really needed me now. I was certain that I had nothing left to offer, that the outcome was entirely in her own hands.

So I shut up and watched, irritated with but unable to prevent my own leaning and turning, shifting and pressing, as if I were out there myself, anticipating, compensating.

When she came to the Grand Curve she was a living flame. Her progress was very slow, but there was a relentless quality to it. Whatever the outcome, I knew that she was being changed, had been changed already, that the Pattern was inscribing itself upon her, and that she was very near to the end of its statement. I almost cried out as she seemed to stop for a moment, but the words died in my throat as she shuddered once, then continued. I wiped my brow on my sleeve as she approached the Final Veil. Whatever the outcome, she had proved her suspicions. Only a child of Amber could have survived as she had.

I do not know how long it took her to pierce the last Veil. Her effort became timeless, and I was caught up in that protracted moment. She was a burning study in extreme slow motion, the nimbus that enshrouded her lighting up the entire chamber like a great blue candle.

And then she was through and onto that final short arc, the last three steps of which may well be the most difficult part of the entire Pattern. Some sort of psychic surface tension seems joined with the physical inertia one encounters just before the point of emergence.

Again, I thought she had stopped, but it was only an appearance. It was like watching someone doing tai chi, the painful slowness of that trio of paces. But she completed it and moved again. If the final step didn't kill her, then she was home free. Then we could talk. . . .

That final moment went on and on and on. Then I saw her foot move forward and depart the Pattern. Shortly, the other foot followed and she stood panting at the center.

"Congratulations!" I shouted.

She waved weakly with her right hand while slowly raising her left to cover her eyes. She stood thus for the better part of a minute, and one who has walked the Pattern understands the feeling. I did not call out again, but let her recover, giving her the silence in which to enjoy her triumph.

The Pattern seemed to be glowing more brightly just then, as it often does immediately after being traversed. This gave a fairyland quality to the grotto—all blue light and shadow—and made a mirror of that small, still pool in the far corner where blind fish swim. I tried to think ahead to what this act might mean, for Coral, for Amber. . . .

She straightened suddenly.

"I'm going to live," she announced.

"Good," I replied. "You have a choice now, you know."

"What do you mean?" she asked.

"You are now in a position to command the Pattern to transport you anywhere," I explained. "So you could just have it deposit you back here again, or you could save yourself a long walk by having it return you to your suite right now. As much as I enjoy your company, I'd recommend the latter since you're probably pretty tired. Then you can soak in a nice warm bath and take your time dressing for dinner. I'll meet you in the dining room. Okay?"

I saw that she was smiling as she shook her head.

"I'm not going to waste an opportunity like this," she said.

"Listen, I know the feeling," I told her. "But I think you should restrain yourself. Rushing off someplace weird could be dangerous, and coming back could be tricky when you haven't had any training in shadow walking."

"It's just sort of a will and expectation thing, isn't it?" she asked. "You kind of impose images on the environment as you go along, don't you?"

"It's trickier than that," I said. "You have to learn to capitalize on certain features as points of departure. Normally, one is accompanied on one's first shadow walk by someone with experience—"

"Okay, I get the idea."

"Not enough," I said. "Ideas are fine, but there's feedback, too. There's a certain feeling you get when it begins working. That can't be taught. It has to be experienced—and until you're sure of it, you should have someone along for a guide."

"Seems like trial and error would do."

"Maybe," I answered. "But supposing you wound up in danger? That'd be a hell of a time to start learning. Kind of distracting—"

"All right. You made your point. Fortunately, I'm not planning on anything that would put me in such a position."

"What are you planning?"

She straightened and gestured widely.

"Ever since I learned about the Pattern, there's been something I wanted to try if I got this far," she said.

"What might that be?"

"I'm going to ask it to send me where I should go."

"I don't understand."

"I'm going to leave the choice up to the Pattern."

I shook my head.

"It doesn't work that way," I told her. "You have to give it an order to transport you."

"How do you know that?"

"It's just the way it works."

"Have you ever tried what I'm saying?"

"No. Nothing would happen."

"Has anyone you know of ever tried it?"

"It would be a waste of time. Look, you're talking as if the Pattern is somehow sentient, is capable of coming to a decision on its own and executing it."

"Yes," she replied. "And it must know me real well after what I've just been through with it. So I'm just going to ask its advice and—"

"Wait!" I said.

"Yes?"

"On the off chance that something happens, how do you plan on getting back?"

"I'll walk, I guess. So you're admitting that something *could* happen?"

"Yes," I said. "It's conceivable that you have an unconscious desire to visit a place, and that it will read that and take you there if you give a transport order. That

won't prove that the Pattern is sentient—just that it's
sensitive. Now, if it were me standing there, I'd be afraid
to take a chance like that. Supposing I have suicidal
tendencies I'm not aware of? Or—"

"You're reaching," she answered. "You're really
reaching."

"I'm just counseling you to play it safe. You have your
whole life to go exploring. It would be silly to—"

"Enough!" she said. "My mind's made up, and that's
it. It feels right. See you later, Merlin."

"Wait!" I cried again. "All right. Do it if you must.
But let me give you something first."

"What?"

"A means of getting out of a tight spot in a hurry.
Here."

I withdrew my Trumps, shuffled out my own card.
Then I unfastened my dagger and sheath from my belt. I
wrapped my card around the haft and tied it there with
my handkerchief.

"You have an idea how to use a Trump?"

"You just stare and think of the person till there's
contact, don't you?"

"That'll do," I said. "Here's mine. Take it with you.
Call me when you want to come home, and I'll bring you
back."

I tossed it out across the Pattern, underhand. She
caught it easily and hung it on her belt on the side
opposite her own.

"Thanks," she said, straightening. "I guess I'll give it
a try now."

"Just in case it really works, don't stay long. Okay?"

"Okay," she answered, and she closed her eyes.

An instant later she was gone. Oh, my.

I moved to the edge of the Pattern and held my hand
above it until I could feel the forces stirring there.

"You'd better know what you're doing," I said. "I
want her back."

A spark shot upward and tickled my palm.

"You trying to tell me you're really sentient?"

Everything swirled about me. The dizziness passed in an instant, and the first thing I noticed then was that the lantern was beside my right foot. When I looked about I realized that I was standing on the other side of the Pattern from where I had been and was now near the door.

"I was within your field and I'm already attuned," I said. "It was just my unconscious desire to get out."

Then I hefted the lantern, locked the door behind me, and hung the key back on its hook. I still didn't trust the thing. If it had really wanted to be helpful, it would have sent me directly to my quarters and saved me all those stairs.

I hurried along the tunnel. It was by far the most interesting first date I'd ever had.

CHAPTER 6

As I passed out of the main hall and headed along the back hallway which would take me to any of a number of stairs, a fellow in black leathers and various pieces of rusty and shiny chain emerged from a corridor to my right, halted, and stared at me. His hair was of an orange Mohawk cut and there were several silver rings in his left ear near what looked like an electrical outlet of some sort.

"Merlin?" he said. "You okay?"

"For the moment," I replied as I drew nearer, trying to place him, there in the dimness.

"Martin!" I said. "You're . . . changed."

He chuckled.

"I'm just back from a very interesting shadow," he said. "Spent over a year there—one of those places where time runs like hell."

"I'd judge—just guessing—that it was high-tech, urban. . . ."

"Right."

"I thought you were a country boy."

"I got over it. Now I know why my dad likes cities and noise."

"You a musician, too?"

"Some. Different sounds, though. You going to be at dinner?"

"I was planning on it. As soon as I get cleaned up and changed."

"See you there, then. We've a lot of things to talk about."

"Sure thing, Cousin."

He clasped my shoulder and released it as I passed. His grip was still strong.

I walked on. Before I'd gone very far, I felt the beginning of a Trump contact. I halted and reached quickly, figuring it was Coral wanting to return. Instead, my eyes met those of Mandor, who smiled faintly.

"Ah, very good," he said. "You are alone and apparently safe."

As things came clearer I saw that Fiona was standing beside him, standing very close as a matter of fact.

"I'm okay," I said. "I'm back in Amber. You all right?"

"Intact," he said, looking past me, though there was not much to see beyond wall and a bit of tapestry.

"Would you care to come through?" I asked.

"I'd love to see Amber," he replied. "But that pleasure will have to await another occasion. We are somewhat occupied at the moment."

"You've discovered the cause of the disturbances?" I asked.

He glanced at Fiona, then back at me.

"Yes and no," he said. "We've some interesting leads but no certainty at the moment."

"Uh, what can I do for you then?" I asked.

Fiona extended her index finger and suddenly became much clearer. I realized that she must have reached out and touched my Trump for better contact.

"We've had an encounter with a manifestation of that machine you built," she said. "Ghostwheel."

"Yes?" I said.

"You're right, it's sentient—social AI as well as technical."

"I was already certain it could pass the Turing test."

"Oh, no doubt about that," she responded, "since by

definition the Turing test requires a machine capable of lying to people and misleading them."

"What are you getting at, Fiona?" I asked.

"It's not just social AI. It's downright antisocial," she replied. "I think your machine is crazy."

"What did it do?" I asked. "Attack you?"

"No, nothing physical. It's wacky and mendacious and insulting, and we're too busy to go into details right now. I'm not saying it couldn't get nasty, though. I don't know. We just wanted to warn you not to trust it."

I smiled.

"That's it? End of message?" I said.

"For now," she answered, lowering her finger and growing dim.

I shifted my gaze to Mandor and was about to explain that I had built a host of safeguards into the thing, so that not just anybody could access it. Mainly, though, I wanted to tell him about Jurt. But our communication was suddenly severed, as I felt another presence reaching toward me.

I was intrigued by the sensation. I had occasionally wondered what would occur if someone tried for a Trump contact when I was already in touch with someone else via a Trump. Would it turn into a conference call? Would someone get a busy signal? Would it put the other party on hold? I'd doubted I'd ever find out, though. It just seemed statistically unlikely. However. . . .

"Merlin, baby. I'm okay."

"Luke!"

Mandor and Fiona were definitely gone.

"I'm really okay now, Merle."

"You sure?"

"Yeah, as soon as I started coming down I switched to a fast lane. In this shadow it's been several days since I've seen you."

He was wearing sunglasses and green swim trunks. He was seated at a small table beside a swimming pool in the shade of a great umbrella, the remains of a large lunch spread before him. A lady in a blue bikini dived into the pool and passed from my line of sight.

"Well, I'm glad to hear about that and—"

"So what happened to me, anyhow? I remember you said something about someone slipping me some acid when I was a prisoner back at the Keep. Is that how it went?"

"It seems very likely."

"I guess that's what happens when you drink the water," he mused. "Okay. What's been going on while I've been out of it?"

Knowing how much to tell him was always a problem. So, "Where do we stand?" I asked.

"Oh. That," he said.

"Yeah."

"Well, I've had a chance to do a lot of thinking," he replied, "and I'm going to call it quits. Honor has been satisfied. It's pointless to keep pushing this thing against everybody else. But I'm not about to put myself in Random's hands for a kangaroo trial. Now it's your turn: Where do I stand so far as Amber's concerned? Should I be looking over my shoulder?"

"Nobody's said anything yet, one way or the other. But Random is out of town now and I just got back myself. I haven't really had a chance to learn what the others' feelings might be on this thing."

He removed his sunglasses and studied me.

"The fact that Random's out of town. . . ."

"No, I know he's not after you," I said, "because he's in Kash—" and I tried to stop it just a syllable too late.

"Kashfa?"

"So I understand."

"What the hell's he doing there? Amber was never interested in the place before."

"There's been a . . . death," I explained. "Some kind of shake-up going on."

"Ha!" Luke remarked. "That bastard finally bought it.

Good! But. . . . Hey! Why's Amber moving in so suddenlike, huh?"

"Don't know," I said.

He chuckled. "Rhetorical question," he said. "I can see what's going on. I've got to admit Random's got style. Listen, when you find out who he puts on the throne let me know, will you? I like to keep abreast of doings in the old hometown."

"Oh, sure," I said, trying unsuccessfully to determine whether such information could be harmful. It would become public knowledge very soon, if it wasn't already.

"So what else is going on? That other person who was Vinta Bayle . . . ?"

"Gone," I said. "I don't know where."

"Very strange," he mused. "I don't think we've seen the last of her. She *was* Gail, too. I'm sure. Let me know if she comes back, will you?"

"Okay. You want to ask her out again?"

He shrugged, then smiled. "I could think of worse ways to spend some time."

"You're lucky she didn't try to take *you* out, literally."

"I'm not so sure she would've," he replied. "We always got along pretty well. Anyhow, none of this is the main reason I called. . . ."

I nodded, having already guessed as much.

"How's my mother doing?" he asked.

"Hasn't stirred," I answered. "She's safe."

"That's something," he said. "You know, it's kind of undignified for a queen to be in that position. A coatrack. Jeez!"

"I agree," I agreed. "But what's the alternative?"

"Well, I'd sort of like to . . . get her freed," he said. "What'll it take?"

"You raise a very thorny issue," I stated.

"I sort of figured that."

"I've a strong feeling she's the one behind this revenge business, Luke, that she's the one who put you up to going after everybody. Like with that bomb. Like encouraging you to set up that private army with modern weapons, to use against Amber. Like trying for a hit on me every spring. Like—''

"Okay, okay. You're right. I don't deny it. But things have changed—''

"Yeah. Her plans fell through and we've got her.''

"That's not what I meant. I'm changed. I understand her now, and I understand myself better. She can't push me around that way anymore.''

"Why is that?''

"That trip I was on. . . . It shook loose my thinking quite a bit. About her and me. I've had several days now to mull over what some of it meant, and I don't think she can pull the same crap on me that she used to.''

I recalled the red-haired woman tied to the stake, tormented by demons. There was a resemblance, now I thought of it.

"But she's still my mother,'' he went on, "and I don't like leaving her in the position she's in. What kind of deal might be possible for turning her loose?''

"I don't know, Luke,'' I answered. "The matter hasn't come up yet.''

"Well, she's *your* prisoner, actually.''

"But her plans were directed against all of us.''

"True, but I won't be helping her with them anymore. She really needs someone like me for carrying them out.''

"Right. And if she doesn't have you to help, what's to prevent her from finding someone like you, as you put it? She'd still be dangerous if we let her go.''

"But you know about her now. That would crimp her style quite a bit.''

"It might just make her more devious.''

He sighed. "I suppose there's some truth in that,'' he admitted. "But she's as venal as most people. It's just a matter of finding the right price.''

"I can't see Amber buying someone off that way.''

"I can.''

"Not when that person is already a prisoner here."

"That does complicate matters a little," he acknowledged. "But I hardly think it's an insurmountable barrier. Not if she's more useful to you free than as a piece of furniture."

"You've lost me," I said. "What are you proposing?"

"Nothing yet. I'm just sounding you out."

"Fair enough. But offhand, I can't see a situation such as you describe arising. More valuable to us free than a prisoner. . . . I guess we'd go where the value lies. But these are just words."

"Just trying to plant a seed or two while I work on it. What is your greatest concern right now?"

"Me? Personally? You really want to know?"

"You bet."

"Okay. My mad brother Jurt has apparently allied himself with the sorcerer Mask back at the Keep. The two of them are out to get me. Jurt made an attempt just this afternoon, but I can see it's really a challenge from Mask. I'm going to take them on soon."

"Hey, I didn't know you had a brother!"

"Half-brother. I have a couple of others, too. But I can get along with them. Jurt's been after me for a long time."

"That's really something. You never mentioned them."

"We never talked family. Remember?"

"Yeah. But you've got me puzzled now. Who's this Mask? I seem to remember your mentioning him before. It's really Sharu Garrul, isn't it?"

I shook my head.

"When I brought your mother out of the citadel she left the company of a similarly stricken old guy with RINALDO carved on his leg. I was trading spells with Mask at the time."

"Most strange," Luke said. "Then he's a usurper. And he's the one slipped me the acid?"

"That seems most likely."

"Then I have a score to settle with him, too—apart from what he did to my mother. How tough is Jurt?"

"Well, he's nasty. But he's kind of clumsy, too. At least, he's screwed up whenever we've fought and left a piece of himself behind."

"He could also be learning from his mistakes, you know."

"That's true. And he said something kind of cryptic today, now you mention it. He talked as if he were about to become very powerful."

"Uh-oh," Luke said. "Sounds as if this Mask is using him as a guinea pig."

"For what?"

"The Fount of Power, man. There's a steady, pulsing source of pure energy inside the Citadel, you know. Inter-Shadow stuff. Comes from the four worlds jamming together there."

"I know. I've seen it in action."

"I've got a feeling that this Mask is still in the process of getting a handle on it."

"He had a pretty good grip when we met."

"Yeah, but there's more to it than plugging into a wall outlet. There are all sorts of subtleties he's probably just becoming aware of and exploring."

"Such as?"

"Bathing a person in it will, if he's properly protected, do wonders for strength, stamina, and magical abilities. That part's easy for a person with some training to learn. I've been through it myself. But old Sharu's notes were in his lab, and there was something more in them—a way of replacing part of the body with energy, really packing it in. Very dangerous. Easily fatal. But if it works you get something special, a kind of superman, a sort of living Trump."

"I've heard that term before, Luke. . . ."

"Probably," he replied. "My father undertook the process, with himself as the subject—"

"That's it!" I said. "Corwin claimed that Brand had

become some sort of living Trump. Made it almost impossible to nail him."

Luke gritted his teeth.

"Sorry," I said. "But that's where I heard about it. So *that* was the secret of Brand's power. . . ."

Luke nodded.

"I get the impression this Mask thinks he knows how it was done and is getting ready to try it on your brother."

"Shit!" I observed. "That's all I need. Jurt as a magical being or a natural force—or whatever the hell. This is serious. How much do you know about the process?"

"Oh, I know most of it, in theory. I wouldn't mess with it, though. I think it takes away something of your humanity. You don't much give a shit about other people or human values afterward. I think that's part of what happened to my father."

What could I say? Maybe that part was true and maybe it wasn't. I was sure Luke wanted to believe in some external cause for his father's treachery. I knew I'd never contradict him on it, even if I learned differently. And so I laughed.

"With Jurt," I said, "there'd be no way of telling the difference."

Luke smiled. Then, "You could get dead going up against a guy like that, along with a sorcerer, on their own turf."

"What choice have I got?" I asked. "They're after me. Better to move now. Jurt hasn't had the treatment yet. Does it take long?"

"Well, there are fairly elaborate preliminaries, but the subject doesn't have to be present for some of them. It all depends on how far along Mask is with the work."

"I'd better move pretty fast then."

"I won't have you going in there alone," he said. "It could be suicide. I know the place. I also have a small force of mercs bivouacked in Shadow and ready for action on short notice. If we can get them in, they can hold off the guards, maybe even take them out."

"Will that fancy ammo work there?"

"No. We tried it when I pulled the glider attack. It'll have to be hand to hand. Body armor and machetes, maybe. I'll have to work it out."

"*We* could use the Pattern to get in, but the troops can't . . . and Trumps aren't reliable for that place."

"I know. I'll have to work on that, too."

"Then it would be you and me against Jurt and Mask. If I tell any of the others here, they'll try to stop me till Random gets back, and that may be too late."

He smiled. "You know, my mother would really be useful in there," he said. "She knows more about the Fount than I do."

"No!" I said. "She tried to kill me."

"Easy, man. Easy," he said. "Hear me out."

"Besides, she lost to Mask last time they met. That's why she's a coatrack."

"All the more reason for her to be wary now. Anyway, it had to be trickery, not skill. She's good. Mask must have surprised her. She'd be a real asset, Merle."

"No! She wants all of us dead!"

"Details," he explained. "After Caine, the rest of you are just symbolic enemies. Mask is a real one, who took something away from her and still has it. Given the choice, she'll go after Mask."

"And if we're successful, she'll turn on Amber afterward."

"Not at all," he said. "That's the beauty of my plan."

"I don't want to hear about it."

"Because you already know you'll agree, right? I just figured a way to solve all your problems. Give her the Keep after it's liberated, as a kind of peace offering, to forget her differences with you guys."

"Just hand her this terrible power?"

"If she were going to use it against you, she'd have done it a long time ago. She's afraid to employ it in the extreme. With Kashfa down the tubes, she'll grab at the chance to salvage something. That's where the value lies."

"You really think so?"

"Better Queen of the Keep than a coatrack in Amber."

"Damn you, Luke. You always make the stupidest things sound sort of attractive."

"It's an art," he replied. "What do you say?"

"I've got to think about it," I said.

"Better think fast, then. Jurt may be bathing in that glow right now."

"Don't pressure me, man. I said I'll think about it. This is only one of my problems. I'm going to eat dinner now and mull things over."

"Want to tell me about your other problems, too? Maybe I can work them into the package some way."

"No, damn it! I'll call you back . . . soon. Okay?"

"Okay. But I'd better be around when you snap Mom out of it, to kind of smooth things over. You *have* figured out how to break the spell, haven't you?"

"Yes."

"Glad to know that. I wasn't sure how to do it, and I can stop working on it now. I'm going to finish here and go shape up the troops," he said, eyeing the lady in the bikini who had just emerged from the pool. "Call me."

"Okay," I said, and he was gone.

Damn. Amazing. No wonder Luke kept winning those sales awards. I had to admit it was a good pitch, despite my feelings about Jasra. And Random had not ordered me to keep her a prisoner. Of course, he had not had much opportunity to tell me anything the last time we had been together. Would she really behave as Luke said, though? It made a sort of sense, but then people seldom keep company with rationality at times when they should.

I passed along the hallway and decided to use the back stair. As I made the turn, I saw that there was a figure standing near the top. It was a woman, and she was looking the other way. She had on a full-length red-and-yellow gown. Her hair was very dark and she had lovely shoulders. . . .

She turned when she heard my tread, and I saw that it was Nayda. She studied my face.

"Lord Merlin," she said, "can you tell me where my sister is? I understand she went off with you earlier."

"She was admiring some art, and then she had a little errand she wanted to run afterward," I replied. "I'm not sure exactly where she was going, but she gave the impression she'd be back pretty soon."

"All right," she said. "It's just that it's getting near to dinnertime, and we'd expected her to be joining us. Did she enjoy her afternoon?"

"I believe she did," I said.

"She's been a bit moody recently. We were hoping this trip would cheer her up. She was looking forward to it quite a bit."

"She seemed pretty cheerful when I left her," I admitted.

"Oh, where was that?"

"Near here," I said.

"Where all did you go?"

"We had a long walk in and about town," I explained. "I showed her a bit of the palace, also."

"Then she's in the palace right now?"

"She was the last time I saw her. But she might have stepped out."

"I see," she said. "I'm sorry I didn't really get to talk to you at any length earlier. I feel as if I've known you for a long while."

"Oh?" I said. "Why is that?"

"I read through your file several times. It's kind of fascinating."

"File?"

"It's no secret that we keep files on people we're likely to encounter in our line of work. There's a file on everyone in the House of Amber, of course, even those who don't have much to do with diplomacy."

"I'd never thought about it," I said, "but it figures."

"Your early days are glossed over, of course, and your recent troubles are very confusing."

"They're confusing to me, too," I said. "You trying to update the file?"

"No, just curious. If your problems have ramifications that may involve Begma, we have an interest in them."

"How is it that you know of them at all?"

"We have very good intelligence sources. Small kingdoms often do."

I nodded.

"I won't press you on your sources, but we're not having a fire sale on classified data."

"You misunderstand me," she said. "I'm not trying to update that file either. I was trying to discover whether I might be able to offer you assistance."

"Thank you. I appreciate that," I told her. "I can't really think of any way you could help me, though."

She smiled, showing what seemed a set of perfect teeth.

"I can't be more precise without knowing more," she said. "But if you decide that you do want help—or if you just want to talk—come and see me."

"Well taken," I said. "I'll see you at dinner."

"Later, too, I hope," she said, as I passed her and turned down the hall.

What had she meant by that last bit? I wondered. Was she talking assignation? If so, her motives seemed awfully transparent. Or was she merely expressing her desire for information? I was not certain.

As I passed along the hallway in the direction of my rooms I noted an odd lighting phenomenon ahead of me: A bright white band about six or eight inches in width ran up both walls, across the ceiling, and over the floor. I slowed as I neared it, wondering whether someone had introduced a new method of illuminating the place in my absence.

As I stepped over the band on the floor, everything

disappeared, except for the light itself, which resolved into a perfect circle, flipped once about me and settled on a level with my feet, myself at its center. The world appeared beyond the circle, suddenly, and it looked as if it were made of green glass formed into a dome. The surface on which I stood was reddish, irregular and moist in the pale light. It was not until a large fish swam by that I realized I might be underwater, standing on a ridge of coral.

"This is pretty as all hell," I said, "but I was trying to get to my apartment."

"Just showing off a bit," came a familiar voice which sounded eerily all about my magic circle. "Am I a god?"

"You can call yourself whatever you want," I said. "Nobody will disagree with you."

"It might be fun being a god."

"Then what does that make me?" I asked.

"That's a difficult theological question."

"Theological, my ass. I'm a computer engineer, and you know I built you, Ghost."

A sound like a sigh filled my submarine cell.

"It's hard to get away from one's roots."

"Why try? What's wrong with roots? All of the best plants have them."

"Pretty bloom above, mire and muck below."

"In your case it's metal and an interesting cryogenic setup—and quite a few other things—all of them very clean."

"Maybe it's mire and muck that I need, then."

"You feeling all right, Ghost?"

"I'm still trying to find myself."

"Everyone goes through phases like that. It'll pass."

"Really?"

"Really."

"When? How? Why?"

"It would be cheating to tell. Besides, it's different for everyone."

A whole school of fish swam by—little black-and-red-striped guys.

"I can't quite swing the omniscience business . . ." Ghost said after a time.

"That's okay. Who needs it?" I said.

". . . And I'm still working on omnipotence."

"That one's hard, too," I agreed.

"You're very understanding, Dad."

"I try. You got any special problems?"

"You mean, apart from the existential?"

"Yeah."

"No. I brought you here to warn you about a fellow named Mandor. He's—"

"He's my brother," I said.

There was silence.

Then, "That would make him my uncle, wouldn't it?"

"I guess so."

"How about the lady with him? She—"

"Fiona's my aunt."

"*My* great-aunt. Oh, my!"

"What's wrong?"

"It's bad form to speak ill of relatives, isn't it?"

"Not in Amber," I said. "In Amber we do it all the time."

The circle of light flipped again. We were back in the hallway.

"Now that we're in Amber," he said, "I want to speak ill of them. I wouldn't trust them if I were you. I think they're a little crazy. Also insulting and mendacious."

I laughed. "You're becoming a true Amberite."

"I am?"

"Yes. That's the way we are. Nothing to worry about. What came down between you, anyhow?"

"I'd rather work it out on my own, if you don't mind."

"Whatever you think is best."

"I don't really need to warn you about them?"

"No."

"Okay. That was my main concern. I guess I'll go and try the mire and muck bit now—"

"Wait!"

"What?"

"You seem pretty good at transporting things through Shadow these days."

"I seem to be improving, yes."

"What about a small band of warriors and their leader?"

"I think I could manage that."

"And me."

"Of course. Where are they and where do you want to go?"

I fished in my pocket, found Luke's Trump, held it up before me.

"But . . . He's the one you warned me not to trust," Ghost said.

"It's okay now," I told him. "Just for this matter. Nothing else, though. Things have changed a bit."

"I don't understand. But if you say so."

"Can you run him down and set things up?"

"I should be able to. Where do you want to go?"

"Do you know the Keep of the Four Worlds?"

"Yes. But that's a dangerous place, Dad. Very tricky coming and going. And that's where the red-haired lady tried to lay a power lock on me."

"Jasra."

"I never knew her name."

"She's Luke's mother," I explained, waving his Trump.

"Bad blood," Ghost stated. "Maybe we shouldn't have anything to do with either of them."

"She might be coming with us," I said.

"Oh, no. That's a dangerous lady. You don't want her along. Especially not in a place where she's strong. She might try to grab me again. She might succeed."

"She'll be too occupied with other matters," I said,

"and I may need her. So start thinking of her as part of the package."

"Are you sure you know what you're doing?"

"I'm afraid so."

"When do you want to go there?"

"That depends in part on when Luke's troops will be ready. Why don't you go and find out?"

"All right. But I still think you might be making a mistake, going into that place with those people."

"I need someone who can help, and the die is damned well cast," I said.

Ghost coalesced to a point and winked out.

I drew a deep breath, changed my mind about sighing, and moved on toward my nearest door, which was not that much farther up the hall. As I was reaching for it I felt the movement of a Trump contact. Coral?

I opened myself to it. Mandor appeared before me again.

"Are you all right?" he asked immediately. "We were cut off in such an odd fashion."

"I'm fine," I told him. "We were cut off in a once-in-a-lifetime fashion. Not to worry."

"You seem a trifle agitated."

"That's because it's an awfully long walk from downstairs to upstairs with all the powers of the universe converging to slow me."

"I don't understand."

"It's been a rough day," I said. "See you later."

"I did want to talk with you some more, about those storms and the new Pattern and—"

"Later," I said. "I'm waiting on an incoming call."

"Sorry. No rush. I'll check back."

He broke the contact and I reached for the latch. I wondered whether it would solve everybody's problems if I could turn Ghost into an answering service.

CHAPTER 7

I hung my cloak on Jasra and my weapons belt on the bedpost. I cleaned my boots, washed my hands and face, hunted up a fancy ivory shirt—all ruffled, brocaded, frogged—and put it on, along with a pair of gray trousers. Then I brushed off my deep purple jacket, the one on which I'd once laid a spell to make the wearer seem a little more charming, witty, and trustworthy than is actually the case. It seemed a good occasion for getting some use out of it.

As I was brushing my hair there came a knock on the door.

"Just a minute," I called.

I finished up—which left me ready to go and also, probably, running late—then went to the door, unbarred it, and opened it.

Bill Roth stood there in browns and reds, looking like an aging condottiere.

"Bill!" I said, clasping his hand, arm, and shoulder and leading him in. "Good to see you. I'm just back from some troubles and about to take off after more. I didn't know whether you were here in the palace now or what. I was going to look you up again as soon as things slowed a bit."

He smiled and punched my shoulder lightly.

"I'll be at dinner," he replied, "and Hendon said you'd be there, too. I thought I'd come up and walk over with you, though, since those Begman people will be there.''

"Oh? You got some news?''

"Yes. Any fresh word on Luke?''

"I was just talking to him. He says the vendetta's off.''

"Any chance of his wanting to justify himself at that hearing you asked me about?''

"Not from the way he sounded.''

"Too bad. I've been doing a lot of research, and there are some good precedents for the vendetta defense—like, there was your uncle Osric, who took on the whole House of Karm over the death of a relative on his mother's side. Oberon was particularly friendly with Karm in those days, too, and Osric offed three of them. Oberon acquitted him at a hearing, though, basing his decision on earlier cases, and he even went further by stating a kind of general rule—''

"Oberon also sent him off to the front lines in a particularly nasty war," I interrupted, "from which he did not return.''

"I wasn't aware of that part," Bill said, "but he did come off well in court.''

"I'll have to mention it to Luke," I said.

"Which part?" he asked.

"Both," I answered.

"That wasn't the main thing I came to tell you," he went on. "There's something going on at a military level.''

"What are you talking about?''

"It's even easier to show you," he explained. "It should only take a minute.''

"Okay. Let's go," I agreed, and I followed him out into the hall.

He led the way down the back stair and turned left at its foot. We moved on past the kitchen and followed another hallway which turned off toward the rear. As we did, I heard some rattling sounds from up ahead. I glanced at Bill, who nodded.

"That's what I heard earlier," he told me, "when I was passing by. That's why I took a walk up this way. Everything around here makes me curious."

I nodded, understanding the feeling. Especially when I knew that the sounds were coming from the main armory.

Benedict stood in the midst of activity, peering at his thumbnail through a rifle barrel. He looked up immediately and our eyes met. Perhaps a dozen men moved about him, carrying weapons, cleaning weapons, stacking weapons.

"I thought you were in Kashfa," I said.

"Was," he replied.

I gave him a chance to continue, but nothing was forthcoming. Benedict has never been noted for loquacity.

"Looks like you're getting ready for something close to home," I remarked, knowing that gunpowder was useless here and that the special ammo we had only worked in the area of Amber and certain adjacent kingdoms.

"Always best to be safe," he said.

"Would you care to elaborate on that?" I asked.

"Not now," he answered, a reply twice as long as I'd anticipated and holding out hope of future enlightenment.

"Should we all be digging in?" I asked. "Fortifying the town? Arming ourselves? Raising—"

"It won't come to that," he said. "Just go on about your business."

"But—"

He turned away. I'd a feeling the conversation was over. I was sure of it when he ignored my next several questions. I shrugged and turned back to Bill.

"Let's go eat," I said.

As we walked back up the hall, Bill said softly, "Any idea what it means?"

"Dalt's in the neighborhood," I told him.

"Benedict was in Begma with Random. Dalt could be causing trouble there."

"I've a feeling he's nearer."

"If Dalt were to capture Random. . . ."

"Impossible," I said, feeling a slight chill at the idea. "Random can trump back here anytime he wants. No. When I talked about defending Amber, and Benedict said, 'It won't come to that,' I got the impression he was talking about something close at hand. Something he feels he can control."

"I see what you mean," he agreed. "But then he told you not to bother fortifying."

"If Benedict feels we don't need to fortify, then we don't need to fortify."

"Waltz and drink champagne while the cannons boom?"

"If Benedict says it's okay."

"You really trust that guy. What would you do without him?"

"Be more nervous," I said.

He shook his head. "Excuse me," he said. "I'm not used to being acquainted with legends."

"You don't believe me?"

"I shouldn't believe you, but I do believe you. That's the trouble." He was silent as we turned the corner and headed back toward the stair. Then he added, "It was that way whenever I was around your father, too."

"Bill," I said, as we began to climb. "You knew my dad back before he regained his memory, when he was just plain old Carl Corey. Maybe I've been going about this thing wrong. Is there anything you can recall about that phase of his life which might explain where he is now?"

He halted a moment and looked at me.

"Don't think I haven't thought about that angle, Merle. Many a time I've wondered whether he might have been involved in something as Corey that he'd have felt obliged to follow through on once his business here was finished. But he was a very secretive man, even in that incarnation. Paradoxical, too. He'd done a lot of hitches in a lot of different varieties of military, which seems logical enough. But he sometimes wrote music, which goes against that hard-ass image.''

"He'd lived a long time. He'd learned a lot, felt a lot.''

"Exactly, and that's what makes it hard to guess what he might have been involved in. Once or twice when he'd had a few drinks he'd mention people in the arts and sciences I'd never have guessed him to be acquainted with. He was never just plain Carl Corey. He had a few centuries' worth of Earth memory when I knew him. That makes for a character too complex to be easily predictable. I just don't know what he might have gone back to—if he went back.''

We continued on up the stairway. Why did I feel that Bill knew more than he was telling me?

I heard music as we neared the dining room, and when we entered, Llewella gave me a nasty look. I saw that food was being kept warm at a serving table off against the far wall, and no one was seated yet. People stood about talking, drinks in hand, and most of them glanced in our direction as we entered. Three musicians were playing, off to my right. The dining table was to my left, near the big window in the south wall, providing a glorious view across the town below. It was still snowing lightly, casting a spectral veil over the entire bright prospect.

Llewella approached quickly.

"You've kept everybody waiting," she whispered. "Where's the girl?''

"Coral?''

"Who else?''

"I'm not sure where she's gotten off to," I said. "We parted company a couple of hours ago.''

"Well, is she coming or isn't she?''

"I'm not sure.''

"We can't keep things waiting any longer," she said. "And now the seating arrangement's screwed. What did you do, wear her out?''

"Llewella. . . ."

She muttered something I didn't understand in some lisping Rebman dialect. Just as well, probably. She turned away then and moved off toward Vialle.

"You in a heap of trouble, boy," Bill commented at my side. "Let's hit the bar while she's reassigning places."

But the wine steward was already approaching with a couple of drinks on a tray.

"Bayle's Best," he observed as we took them.

I sipped and saw that he was right, which heartened me a bit.

"I don't recognize all of these people," Bill said. "Who's that fellow with the red sash, over by Vialle?"

"That's Orkuz, the Begman prime minister," I told him, "and the rather attractive lady in the yellow-and-red dress who's talking to Martin is his daughter Nayda. Coral—the one I just got chewed out about—is her sister."

"Uh-huh. And who's the husky blond lady batting her eyes at Gérard?"

"I don't know," I said. "And I don't know that lady and the guy over to the right of Orkuz either."

We drifted inward, and Gérard, looking perhaps a trifle uncomfortable in layers of ruffled finery, introduced us to the lady he was with as Dretha Gannell, assistant to the Begman ambassador. The ambassador, it turned out, was the tall lady standing near Orkuz—and her name, I gathered, was Ferla Quist. The fellow with her was her secretary, whose name sounded something like Cade. While we were looking in that direction, Gérard tried slipping off and leaving us with Ferla. But she caught his sleeve and asked him something about the fleet. I smiled and nodded and moved away. Bill came along.

"Goodness! Martin's changed!" he announced suddenly. "He looks like a one-man rock video. I almost didn't recognize him. Just last week—"

"It's been over a year," I said, "for him. He's been off finding himself on some street scene."

"I wonder if he's finished?"

"Didn't get a chance to ask him that," I replied, but a peculiar thought occurred to me. I shelved it.

The music died just then, and Llewella cleared her throat and indicated Hendon, who announced the new seating arrangement. I was at the foot of the table, and I learned later that Coral was to have been seated to my left and Cade to my right. I also learned later that Llewella had tried to get hold of Flora at the last minute, to sit in Coral's place, but Flora wasn't taking any calls.

As it was, Vialle, at the head, had Llewella seated to her right and Orkuz to her left, with Gérard, Dretha, and Bill below Llewella, and Ferla, Martin, Cade, and Nayda below Orkuz. I found myself escorting Nayda to the table and seating her to my right, while Bill settled himself at my left.

"Fuss, fuss, fuss," Bill muttered softly, and I nodded, then introduced him to Nayda as counsel to the House of Amber. She looked impressed and asked him about his work. He proceeded to charm her with a story about once having represented the interests of a dog in an estate settlement, which had nothing to do with Amber but was a good story. Got her to laughing a bit, and also Cade, who was listening in.

The first course was served and the musicians began playing again, softly, which shortened the distance our voices carried and reduced conversation to a more intimate level. At this, Bill signaled he had something he wanted to tell me, but Nayda had beaten him by a second or two and I was already listening to her.

"About Coral," she said softly. "Are you sure she's all right? She wasn't feeling ill when you parted—or anything like that—was she?"

"No," I answered. "She seemed healthy enough."

"Strange," she said. "I had the impression she was looking forward to things like this dinner."

"She's obviously taking longer than she'd intended in whatever she's about," I observed.

"What exactly was she about?" Nayda asked. "Where did you part?"

"Here in the palace," I replied. "I was showing her around. She wanted to spend more time with certain features of the place than I could spare. So I came on ahead."

"I don't think she could have forgotten dinner."

"I think she got caught up by the power of an artistic piece."

"So she's definitely on the premises?"

"Now, that's hard to say. As I said before, a person can always step out."

"You mean you're not sure exactly where she is?"

I nodded.

"I'm not certain where she is at this moment," I said. "She could well be back in her room changing her clothes."

"I'll check after dinner," she said, "if she hasn't shown up by then. If that should be the case, will you help me find her?"

"I was planning on looking for her anyway," I answered, "if she doesn't put in an appearance soon."

She nodded and continued eating. Very awkward. Beyond the fact that I didn't want to distress her, I couldn't very well tell her what had happened without its becoming apparent that her sister was indeed an illegitimate daughter of Oberon. At a time such as this, when I had been cautioned about saying anything that might strain relations between Amber and Begma, I was not about to confirm to the daughter of the Begman prime minister the rumor that her mother had had an affair with the late king of Amber. Maybe it was an open secret back in Begma and nobody gave a damn. But maybe it wasn't. I didn't want to disturb Random for advice, partly because he might be extremely occupied in Kashfa just now, but mainly because he might also start asking me about my own immediate plans and problems, and I would not lie to him. That could get me into too much trouble. Such a conversation might well also result in his forbidding my attack on the Keep. The only other person I could tell about Coral and get some sort of official response from, as to how far I might go in informing her family, was Vialle. Unfortunately, Vialle was completely occupied as hostess at the moment.

I sighed and returned to my dinner.

Bill caught my attention and leaned a little in my direction. I leaned a little, too.

"Yes?" I said.

"There were some things I wanted to tell you," he began. "I was hoping for some leisure, some quiet, and some privacy, though."

I chuckled.

"Exactly," he continued. "I believe this is the best we're going to get for a time. Fortunately, voices don't seem to be carrying if one keeps them down. I couldn't make out what you and Nayda were talking about. So it's probably okay, so long as the musicians keep playing."

I nodded, took a few more bites.

"Thing is, the Begmans shouldn't hear about it, on the one hand. But on the other, I feel that perhaps you ought to know, because of your involvement with Luke and Jasra. So what's your schedule? I'd rather tell you later, but if you're going to be tied up, I can give you the gist of it now."

I glanced at Nayda and Cade. They seemed totally occupied with their food, and I didn't think they could overhear us. Unfortunately, I didn't have any sort of sheltering spells hung.

"Go ahead," I whispered from behind my wine glass.

"First," he said, "Random sent me a whole slew of papers to go over. They're the draft of an agreement whereby Amber will grant Kashfa privileged trade status, the same as Begma. So they'll definitely be coming into the Golden Circle."

"I see," I said. "That doesn't come as a complete surprise. But it's good to know for sure what's going on."

He nodded.

"There's a lot more to it, though," he said.

Just then the musicians stopped playing and I could hear voices from all around the table again. I glanced off to the right and saw that a steward had just taken the players a food tray and some wine. They were setting their instruments aside and taking a break. They had probably been playing for some time before I'd arrived and were doubtless due a rest.

Bill chuckled.

"Later," he said.

"Right."

There followed a funny little fruit dish with an amazing sauce. As I spooned it away, Nayda caught my attention with a gesture and I leaned toward her again.

"So what about tonight?" she whispered.

"What do you mean? I said I'd look for her if she doesn't show up."

She shook her head. "I wasn't referring to that," she said. "I meant later. Will you have time to stop by and talk?"

"About what?"

"According to your file you've been in a bit of trouble recently, with someone trying to get you."

I began wondering about that damned file. But, "It's out of date," I said. "Whatever's in there has already been cleared up."

"Really? Then nobody's after you just now?"

"I wouldn't say that," I replied. "The cast of characters keeps changing."

"So somebody still has you marked?"

I studied her face.

"You're a nice lady, Nayda," I said, "but I've got to ask, What is it to you? Everybody has problems. I just have more than usual at the moment. I'll work them out."

"Or die trying?"

"Maybe. I hope not. But what's your interest?"

She glanced at Cade, who seemed busy with his food.

"It is possible that I could help you."

"In what fashion?"

She smiled.

"A process of elimination," she stated.

"Oh? That refers to a person or persons?"

"Indeed."

"You have some special means of going about this sort of business?"

She continued to smile.

"Yes, it's good for removing problems caused by people," she continued. "All I'll need are their names and locations."

"Some sort of secret weapon?"

She glanced at Cade again, since I had raised my voice a bit.

"You might call it that," she answered.

"An interesting proposal," I said. "But you still haven't answered my first question."

"Refresh my memory."

We were interrupted by the wine steward, who came around topping off goblets, and then by another toast. The first had been to Vialle, led by Llewella. This one was proposed by Orkuz, to "the ancient alliance between Amber and Begma." I drank to that, and I heard Bill mutter, "It's going to get a bit more strained."

"The alliance?" I said.

"Yep."

I glanced at Nayda, who was staring at me, clearly expecting a resumption of our sotto voces. Bill noted this, too, and turned away. Just then Cade began talking to Nayda, however, so I finished what was on my plate and took a sip of wine while I waited. In a little while the plate was whisked away, to be replaced shortly by another.

I glanced at Bill who glanced at Nayda and Cade, then said, "Wait for the music."

I nodded. In a sudden moment of silence I overheard Dretha say, "Is it true that King Oberon's ghost is sometimes seen?" Gérard grunted something that sounded like an affirmative just as they were drowned out again. My mind being a lot fuller than my stomach, I kept eating. Cade, trying to be diplomatic or just conversational, turned my way a little later, addressed me and asked my views on the Eregnor situation. He jerked suddenly then and looked at Nayda. I'd a strong feeling she'd just kicked him under the table, which was fine with me because I didn't know what the hell the Eregnor situation was. I muttered something about there being things to be said for both sides of most matters, which seemed diplomatic enough for anything. If it were something barbed, I supposed I could have countered with an innocent-sounding observation about the Begman party's early arrival, but Eregnor might actually be some tedious conversation piece that Nayda didn't want to get into because it would cut off our own discussion. Also, I'd a feeling that Llewella might suddenly materialize and kick me under the table.

A thought hit suddenly then. Sometimes I'm a little slow. Obviously, they had known Random wasn't here, and from what I already knew and from what Bill had just said, they weren't too happy with whatever Random was about in the neighboring kingdom. Their early arrival seemed intended to embarrass us in some fashion. Did that mean that whatever Nayda was offering me was part of some scheme that fitted in with their general diplomatic strategy on this matter? If so, why me? I was a very poor choice, in that I had no say whatsoever concerning Amber's foreign policy. Were they aware of this? They must be, if their intelligence service were as good as Nayda had indicated. I was baffled, and I was half-tempted to ask Bill his views on the Eregnor situation. But then, he might have kicked me under the table.

The musicians, having finished snacking, resumed the entertainment with "Greensleeves," and Nayda and Bill both leaned toward me simultaneously, then glanced up, their gazes meeting. Both smiled.

"Ladies first," Bill said loudly.

She nodded to him.

Then, "Have a chance to think about my offer?" she asked me.

"Some," I said, "but I had a question. Remember?"

"What was it?"

"It's kind of you to want to do me a favor," I said, "but at times such as this, one must be excused for checking the price tag."

"What if I were to say that your good will would be sufficient?"

"What if I were to say that my good will isn't worth much at the policy level here?"

She shrugged. "Small price for a small return. I already knew that. But you're related to everybody in this place. Nothing may ever happen, but it's conceivable that someone might ask your opinion of us. I'd like you to know you have friends in Begma and to feel kindly disposed toward us if that occurred."

I studied her very serious expression. There was more to it than that, and we both knew it. Only I didn't know what might be on the horizon, and she obviously did.

I reached out and stroked her cheek once with the back of my hand.

"I am expected to say something nice about you folks if someone should ask me, that's all, and for this you will go out and kill someone for me if I just supply the particulars. Right?"

"In a word, yes," she replied.

"It makes me wonder why you think you can manage an assassination better than we could. We're old hands at it."

"We have, as you put it, a secret weapon," she said. "But I was thinking that this is a personal matter for you,

not a state matter—and that you might not want any of
the others involved. Also, I can provide a service that will
not be traceable."

Bag of worms time again. Was she implying that she
thought I did not trust all of the others here—or that I
should not? What did she know that I didn't? Or was she
just guessing, based on Amber's history of intrigue within
the family? Or was she intentionally trying to stir up a
generational conflict? Would that suit Begma's purpose in
some fashion? Or. . . . Was she guessing that such a
situation existed and offering to remove a family member
for me? And if so, did she think I'd be stupid enough to
get someone else to do the job? Or even to discuss such
a notion and thereby give Begma a shot at sufficient
evidence to have some kind of hold over me? Or. . . .

I drew back from the view. It pleased me that my
thought processes were finally working properly for the
company my family keeps. (Both my families, actually.)
It had taken me a long while to get the hang of it. It felt
good.

A simple refusal would foreclose all of the above. But,
on the other hand, if I were to string her along a bit, she
might prove a tantalizing source of information.

So, "Would you go after anyone I would name?" I
said. "Anyone?"

She studied my face very carefully. Then, "Yes," she
answered.

"You must excuse me again," I responded, "but doing
it for such an intangible as my good will causes me to
wonder about your good faith."

Her face reddened. Whether it was a simple blush or
anger I could not be certain, because she looked away
immediately. This didn't bother me, though, because I
was certain it was a buyer's market.

I returned my attention to my food and was able to put
away several mouthfuls before she was back again.

"Does this mean you won't be stopping by tonight?"
she asked.

"I can't," I said. "I am going to be completely occupied."

"I can believe you are very busy," she said. "But does that mean we will not be able to talk at all?"

"It depends entirely on how things break," I said. "I have an awful lot going on just now, and I may be leaving town soon."

She started slightly. I was certain she considered asking me where I was going, but thought better of it.

Then, "This is awkward," she said. "Have you refused my offer?"

"Is the deal only good for this evening?" I asked.

"No, but it was my understanding you were in some peril. The sooner you move against your enemy, the sooner your sleep is untroubled."

"You feel I am in danger here in Amber?"

She hesitated a moment, then said, "No one is safe, anywhere, from an enemy of sufficient determination and skill."

"Do you feel the threat to be a local one?" I inquired.

"I asked you to name the party," she stated. "You are in the best position to know."

I drew back immediately. It was too simple an entrapment, and obviously she'd already smelled it.

"You've given me much to think about," I answered, and I returned to my food.

After a time, I saw that Bill was looking at me as if he wanted to say something. I gave him a minuscule shake of my head, which he seemed to understand.

"Breakfast, then?" I heard her say. "This trip you spoke of could represent a time of vulnerability. It would be good to settle this before you depart."

"Nayda," I said, as soon as I had swallowed, "I would like to be clear on the matter of my benefactors. If I were to discuss this with your father—"

"No!" she interrupted. "He knows nothing about it!"

"Thank you. You must admit my curiosity as to the level at which this plan originates."

"There is no need to look any further," she stated. "It is entirely my idea."

"Some of your earlier statements cause me to infer that you have special connections within the Begman intelligence community."

"No," she said, "only the ordinary ones. The offer is my own."

"But someone would have to . . . effectuate this design."

"That is the province of the secret weapon."

"I would have to know more about it."

"I've offered you a service and I've promised you total discretion. I will go no further as to means."

"If this idea is wholly your own, it would seem that you stand to benefit from it personally. How? What's in it for you?"

She looked away. She was silent for a long time.

"Your file," she said at last. "It was . . . fascinating reading it. You're one of the few people here close to my own age, and you've led such an interesting life. You can't imagine how dull most of the things I have to read are—agricultural reports, trade figures, appropriations studies. I have no social life whatsoever. I am always on call. Every party I attend is really a state function in one form or another. I read your file over and over and I wondered about you. I . . . I have something of a crush on you. I know it sounds silly, but it's true. When I saw some of the recent reports and realized that you might be in great danger, I decided I would help you if I could. I have access to all sorts of state secrets. One of them would provide me with the means of helping you. Using it would benefit you without damaging Begma, but it would be disloyal of me to discuss it further. I've always wanted to meet you, and I was very jealous of my sister when you took her out today. And I still wish you'd stop by later."

I stared at her. Then I raised my wineglass to her and took a drink.

"You are . . . amazing," I said. I couldn't think of anything else to say. It was either an on-the-spot fabrication or it was true. If it were true, it was somewhat pathetic; if not, I thought it a rather clever bit of quick thinking, calculated to hit me in that wonderfully vulnerable place, the ego. She deserved either my sympathy or my wariest admiration. So I added, "I'd like to meet the person who wrote the reports. There may be a great creative talent going to waste in a government office."

She smiled, raised her own glass and touched it to mine.

"Think about it," she said.

"I can honestly say I won't forget you," I told her.

We both returned to our food, and I spent the next five minutes or so catching up. Bill decently allowed me to do this. Also, I think, he was waiting to be certain that my conversation with Nayda was finally concluded.

At last he winked at me.

"Got a minute?" he asked.

"Afraid so," I said.

"I won't even ask whether it was business or pleasure going on on the other side."

"It was a pleasure," I said, "but a strange business. Don't ask or I'll miss dessert."

"I'll summarize," he said. "The coronation in Kashfa will take place tomorrow."

"Not wasting any time, are we?"

"No. The gentleman who will be taking the throne is Arkans, Duke of Shadburne. He's been in and out of various Kashfan governments in fairly responsible positions any number of times over the years. He actually knows how things work, and he's distantly related to one of the earlier monarchs. Didn't get along well with Jasra's crowd and pretty much stayed at his country place the whole time she was in power. He didn't bother her and she didn't bother him."

"Sounds reasonable."

"In fact, he actually shared her sentiments on the Eregnor situation, as the Begmans are well aware—"

"Just what," I asked, "is the Eregnor situation?"

"It's their Alsace-Lorraine," he said, "a large, rich area between Kashfa and Begma. It has changed hands back and forth so many times over the centuries that both countries make reasonable-sounding claims to it. Even the inhabitants of the area aren't all that firm on the matter. They have relatives in both directions. I'm not even sure they care which side claims them, so long as their taxes don't go up. I think Begma's claim might be a little stronger, but I could argue the case either way."

"And Kashfa holds it now, and Arkans says they'll damn well keep it."

"Right. Which is the same thing Jasra said. The interim ruler, however—Jaston was his name, military man—was actually willing to discuss its status with the Begmans, before his unfortunate fall from the balcony. I think he wanted to repair the treasury and was considering ceding the area in return for the settlement of some ancient war damage claims. Things were actually well along and headed in that direction."

"And . . . ?" I said.

"In the papers I got from Random, Amber specifically recognizes Kashfa as including the area of Eregnor. Arkans had insisted that go into the treaty. Usually—from everything I've been able to find in the archives—Amber avoids getting involved in touchy situations like this between allies. Oberon seldom went looking for trouble. But Random seems to be in a hurry, and he let this guy drive a hard bargain."

"He's overreacting," I said, "not that I blame him. He remembers Brand too well."

Bill nodded.

"I'm just the hired help," he said. "I don't want to have an opinion."

"Well, anything else I should know about Arkans?"

"Oh, there are lots of other things the Begmans don't

like about him, but that's the big one—right when they thought they were making some headway on an issue that's been a national pastime for generations. They've even gone to war over the matter in the past. Don't doubt that that's why they came rushing to town. Govern yourself accordingly."

He raised his goblet and took a drink.

A little later Vialle said something to Llewella, rose to her feet, and announced that she had to see to something, that she'd be right back. Llewella started to get up also, but Vialle put a hand on her shoulder, whispered something, and departed.

"Wonder what that could be?" Bill said.

"Don't know," I answered.

He smiled.

"Shall we speculate?"

"My mind's on cruise control," I told him.

Nayda gave me a long stare. I met it and shrugged.

Another little while, and plates were cleared and more were coming. Whatever it was looked good. Before I could find out for certain, though, a member of the general house staff entered and approached.

"Lord Merlin," she said, "the queen would like to see you."

I was on my feet immediately.

"Where is she?"

"I'll take you to her."

I excused myself from my companions, borrowing the line that I'd be right back, wondering if it were true. I followed her out and around the corner to a small sitting room, where she left me with Vialle, who was seated in an uncomfortable-looking high-backed chair of dark wood and leather, held together with cast iron studs. If she'd wanted muscle, she'd have sent for Gérard. If she'd wanted a mind full of history and political connivance, Llewella would be here. So I was guessing it involved magic, since I was the authority in residence.

But I was wrong.

"I'd like to speak to you," she said, "concerning a small state of war in which we seem about to become engaged."

CHAPTER 8

After a pleasant time with a pretty lady, a series of stimulating hallway conversations, and a relaxing dinner with family and friends, it seemed almost fitting that it be time for something different and distracting. The idea of a small war seemed, at least, better than a big one, though I did not say that to Vialle. A moment's careful thought, and I shaped the query:

"What's going on?"

"Dalt's men are dug in near the western edge of Arden," she said. "Julian's are strung out facing them. Benedict has taken Julian additional men and weapons. He says he can execute a flanking movement that will take Dalt's line apart. But I told him not to."

"I don't understand. Why not?"

"Men will die," she said.

"That's the way it is in war. Sometimes you have no choice."

"But we do have a choice, of sorts," she said, "one that I don't understand. And I do want to understand it before I give an order that will result in numerous deaths."

"What is the choice?" I asked.

"I came here to respond to a Trump message from Julian," she said. "He had just spoken with Dalt under a flag of truce. Dalt told him that his objective was not, at this time, the destruction of Amber. He pointed out that he could conduct an expensive attack, though, in terms of

136

our manpower and equipment. He said he'd rather save himself and us the expense, however. What he really wants is for us to turn two prisoners over to him—Rinaldo and Jasra.''

"Huh?" I said. "Even if we wanted to, we can't give him Luke. He's not here.''

"That is what Julian told him. He seemed very surprised. For some reason, he believed we had Rinaldo in custody.''

"Well, we're not obliged to provide the man with an education. I gather he's been something of a pain for years. I think Benedict has the right answer for him.''

"I did not call you in for advice,'' she said.

"Sorry," I told her. "It's just that I don't like seeing someone trying to pull a stunt like this and actually believing he has a chance of success.''

"He has no chance of success,'' Vialle stated. "But if we kill him now, we learn nothing. I would like to find out what is behind this.''

"Have Benedict bring him in. I have spells that will open him up.''

She shook her head.

"Too risky," she explained. "Once bullets start flying, there's the chance one might find him. Then we lose even though we win.''

"I don't understand what it is that you want of me.''

"He asked Julian to get in touch with us and relay his demand. He's promised to hold the truce until we give him some sort of official answer. Julian says he has the impression that Dalt would settle for either one of them.''

"I don't want to give him Jasra either.''

"Neither do I. What I do want very badly is to know what is going on. There would be small point in releasing Jasra and asking her, since this is a recent development. I want to know whether you have means of getting in touch with Rinaldo. I want to talk to him.''

"Well, uh . . . yes," I said. "I have a Trump for him.''

"Use it."

I got it out. I regarded it. I moved my mind into that special area of alertness and calling. The picture changed, came alive. . . .

It was twilight, and Luke stood near a campfire. He had on his green outfit, a light brown cloak about his shoulders clasped with that Phoenix pin.

"Merle," he said. "I can move the troops pretty fast. When do you want to hit the place and—"

"Put it on hold," I interrupted. "This is something different."

"What?"

"Dalt's at the gates, and Vialle wants to talk to you before we take him apart."

"Dalt? There? Amber?"

"Yes, yes, and yes. He says he'll go and play someplace else if we give him the two things he wants most in the world: you and your mother."

"That's crazy."

"Yeah. We think so, too. Will you talk to the queen about it?"

"Sure. Bring me thr—" He hesitated and looked into my eyes.

I smiled.

He extended his hand. I reached forward and took it. Suddenly, he was there. He looked about, saw Vialle. Immediately, he unclasped his sword belt and passed it to me. He approached her, dropped to his right knee, and lowered his head.

"Your Majesty," he said. "I've come."

She reached forward and touched him.

"Raise your head," she said.

He did, and her sensitive fingers slid over the planes and arches of his face.

"Strength," she said, "and sorrow. . . . So you're Rinaldo. You've brought us some grief."

"It works both ways, Your Majesty."

"Yes, of course," she replied. "Wrongs done and

wrongs avenged have a way of spilling over on the innocent. How far will it go this time?"

"This thing with Dalt?" he asked.

"No. This thing with you."

"Oh," he said. "It's over. I've done with it. No more bombs or ambushes. I've already told Merlin that."

"You've known him for several years?"

"Yes."

"You've become friends?"

"He's one of the reasons I'm calling it off."

"You must trust him, to come here. I respect that," she said. "Take this."

She removed a ring she wore upon her right forefinger. The band was of gold, the stone a milky green; the prongs of its setting caught it in a fashion to suggest some mantic spider guarding dreamland treasures against the daybreak world.

"Your Majesty. . . ."

"Wear it," she said.

"I will," he replied, slipping it upon the little finger of his left hand. "Thank you."

"Rise. I want you to know exactly what has occurred."

He got to his feet, and she began telling him what she had told me, concerning Dalt's arrival, his forces' disposition, his demands, while I stood stunned at the implications of what she had done. She had just placed Luke under her protection. Everyone in Amber knew that ring. I wondered what Random would think. I realized then that there would not be a hearing. Poor Bill. I believe he was really looking forward to arguing Luke's case.

"Yes, I know Dalt," I heard him saying. "Once we shared . . . certain goals. But he's changed. He tried to kill me the last time we met. I'm not sure why. At first I thought the wizard of the Keep had taken control of him."

"And now?"

"Now, I just don't understand. I've a feeling he's on a leash, but I don't know who holds it."

"Why not the wizard?"

"It makes no sense to go to these lengths to claim me when he had me and let me go just a few days ago. He could simply have left me in my cell."

"True," she replied. "What is this wizard's name?"

"Mask," he answered. "Merlin knows more about him than I do."

"Merlin," she said. "Who is this Mask?"

"He's the wizard who took the Keep of the Four Worlds away from Jasra," I explained, "who, in turn, had taken it away from Sharu Garrul, who is now also a coatrack. Mask wears a blue mask and seems to draw power from a strange fountain in the citadel there. Doesn't seem to like me much either. That's about all I can tell you."

I'd omitted mentioning my plan to head that way for a showdown soon, because of Jurt's involvement, for the same reason I hadn't wanted Random to know about it. I was certain Luke had tossed me the question because he wasn't sure how far I wanted it taken.

"That doesn't really tell us much," she decided, "as to Dalt's involvement."

"There may not be a connection," I said. "I gather Dalt is a mercenary, and their relationship could have been a one-time thing. He could either be working for someone else now or pulling something on his own."

"I can't see why anybody wants us badly enough to go to such dramatic lengths," Luke said. "But I've a score to settle with that guy, and I'm going to combine business with pleasure."

"What do you mean?" she asked.

"I assume there's a way to get down there in a hurry," he said.

"One could always trump through to Julian," I said, "but what have you got in mind, Luke?"

"I want to talk to Dalt."

"It's too dangerous," she said, "since you're what he wants."

Luke grinned. "It could be a bit dangerous for Dalt, too," he replied.

"Wait a minute," I said. "If you've got more in mind than just talking, you could blow this truce. Vialle's trying to avoid a conflict here."

"There won't be any conflict," Luke said. "Look, I've known Dalt since we were kids, and I think he's bluffing. He does that sometimes. He hasn't got the kind of force to risk another attack on Amber. Your guys would slaughter him. If he wants Mom or me, I think he'd be willing to tell me why, and that's what we want to find out, isn't it?"

"Well, yes," I said. "But—"

"Let me go," he said to Vialle, "and I'll find a way to get him off your back. I promise."

"You tempt me," she told him. "But I don't like your talk of settling accounts with him at this time. As Merlin said, I want to avoid this conflict—for more than one reason."

"I promise not to let it go that far," he stated. "I can read the dice. I'm good at playing things by ear. I'm willing to postpone gratification."

"Merlin . . . ?" she said.

"He's right, in that," I answered. "He's the deadliest salesman in the southwest."

"I'm afraid I don't understand the concept."

"It's a highly specialized art, back on that Shadow Earth we both inhabited. In fact, he's using it on you right now."

"Do you think he can do what he says?"

"I think he's very good at getting what he wants."

"Exactly," Luke observed. "And since we both want the same thing here, I think the future looks bright for all of us."

"I see what you mean," she said. "How much danger would this put you near, Rinaldo?"

"I'll be as safe as I am right here in Amber," he said. She smiled.

"All right, I'll speak to Julian," she agreed, "and you can go to him and see what you can learn from Dalt."

"A moment," I requested. "It's been snowing on and off, and that's a pretty nasty wind out there. Luke just came in from a more temperate clime, and it's a pretty flimsy-looking cloak he has on. Let me get him something warmer. I've a nice heavy one he can take, if he finds it suitable."

"Go ahead," she said.

"We'll be right back."

She pursed her lips, then nodded.

I passed Luke his weapons belt and he buckled it on. I knew that she knew I just wanted to talk to him alone for a few minutes. And she was certainly aware that I knew it. And we both knew she trusted me, which brightens my existence, as well as complicating it.

As we passed along the hallway toward my rooms, I'd intended to fill Luke in concerning the upcoming coronation in Kashfa, as well as a few other matters. I waited, however, till we were well away from the sitting room, because Vialle has inordinately acute hearing. This, though, gave Luke a foot in the door, and he began to speak first.

"What a strange development," he said. Then, "I like her, but I've a feeling she knows more than she's telling."

"Probably true," I answered. "I guess we're all like that."

"You, too?"

"These days, yes. It's gotten that way."

"You know anything more about this situation that I should be aware of?"

I shook my head. "This is very new, and she gave you the whole story I know. Would you, perchance, know something about it that we don't?"

"Nope," he said. "It came as a surprise to me, too. But I've got to pursue it."

"I guess so."

We were nearing my stretch of corridor now, and I felt obliged to prepare him.

"We'll be to my rooms in a minute," I said, "and I just wanted you to know your mother's in there. She's safe, but you won't find her too talkative."

"I'm familiar with the results of that spell," he said. "I also recall that you said you know how to lift it. So. . . . That leads into the next topic. I've been thinking. This interlude is slowing us down a bit in our plan for going after Mask and your brother."

"Not all that much," I responded.

"We don't really know how long this is going to take me, though," he went on. "Supposing it drags out a bit? Or supposing something happens to really slow me down?"

I gave him a quick glance.

"Like, what have you got in mind?" I asked.

"I don't know. I'm just supposing. Okay? I like to plan ahead. Say we get delayed on this attack. . . ."

"All right. Say that," I said, as we neared my door.

"What I'm getting at," he continued, "is, what if we get there too late? Supposing we arrive and your brother has already undergone the ritual that turns him into hell on wheels?"

I unlocked my door, opened it, and held it for him. I did not like entertaining the possibility he had just described, because I recalled my father's stories of the times he'd encountered Brand and faced that uncanny power.

Luke stepped inside. I snapped my fingers and a number of oil lamps came to life, their flames dancing for a moment before settling to a glowing steadiness.

Jasra was there in plain sight before him, holding a number of my garments on outstretched arms. I was concerned for a moment as to what his reaction might be.

He halted, studying her, then advanced, his speculations concerning Jurt forgotten. He regarded her for perhaps ten seconds, and I found myself growing uncomfortable. Then he chuckled.

"She always liked being decorative," he said, "but to combine it with being useful was generally beyond her. You've got to hand it to Mask, even though she probably won't catch the moral of it."

He turned away and faced me.

"No, she'll probably wake up mean as cat piss and looking for trouble," he reflected. Then, "She doesn't seem to be holding that cloak you mentioned."

"I'll get it."

I moved to an armoire, opened it, and fetched out a dark fur one. As we traded, he ran his hand over it.

"Manticore?" he asked.

"Dire wolf," I said.

I hung his within and closed the door while he donned mine.

"As I was saying when we came in here," he offered, "supposing I don't come back?"

"You weren't saying that," I corrected.

"Not in so many words," he admitted. "But whether it's a small delay or the big one, what difference does it make? The point is, what if Jurt goes through with the ritual and succeeds in obtaining the powers he's after before we can do anything about it? And supposing I'm not around right then to give you a hand?"

"That's a lot of supposing," I said.

"That's what separates us from the losers, man. Nice cloak."

He moved toward the door, glanced back at me, at Jasra.

"Okay," I said. "You go down there, Dalt cuts off your head and uses it for a football, then Jurt shows up ten feet tall and farting fire. I'm supposing. How does that separate us from the losers?"

He stepped out into the hall. I followed him, snapping my fingers again, leaving Jasra to the darkness.

"It's a matter of knowing your options," he told me, as I secured the door.

I fell into step beside him as he headed back down the hall.

"A person who acquires that kind of power also picks up a vulnerability, by way of its source," he said.

"What does that mean?" I asked.

"Specifically, I don't know," he told me. "But the power in the Keep can be used against a person who is empowered by the Keep. I learned that much in Sharu's notes. But Mom took them away before I read them all, and I never saw them again. Never trust—that's her motto, I think."

"You're saying . . . ?"

"I'm saying that if something happens to me and he comes up a winner in this game, I believe she knows some special way of destroying him."

"Oh."

"I'm also pretty sure that she'll have to be asked very nicely."

"Somehow, I think I already knew that."

He gave a humorless chuckle.

"So you tell her that I've ended the vendetta, that I'm satisfied, and then offer her the citadel in return for her help."

"What if she says that's not enough?"

"Hell! Turn her back into a coatrack then! It's not as if the guy can't be killed. My dad still died with an arrow through his throat, despite his fancy powers. A death-stroke is still a deathstroke. It's just that delivering it to a guy like that is a lot harder."

"You really think that'll be enough?" I said.

He halted and looked at me, frowning.

"She'll argue, but of course she'll agree," he said. "It'll be a step up in the world. And she'll want revenge on Mask as much as that piece of her former holdings. But to answer your question, don't trust her. No matter what she promises, she'll never be happy with less than she had before. She'll be scheming. She'll be a good ally till the job's done. Then you've got to think about protecting yourself against her. Unless. . . ."

"Unless what?"

"Unless I come up with something to sweeten the pot."

"Like what?"

"I don't know yet. But don't lift that spell until things are definitely settled between Dalt and me. Okay?"

He resumed walking.

"Wait a minute," I said "What are you planning?"

"Nothing special," he answered. "Like I told the queen, I'm just going to play things by ear."

"I sometimes get the feeling you're as devious as you make her out to be," I said.

"I hope so," he replied. "But there's a difference. I'm honest."

"I don't know that I'd buy a used car from you, Luke."

"Every deal I make is special," he said, "and for you it's always top of the line."

I glanced at him, saw that he kept his expression under control.

"What else can I say?" he added, indicating the sitting room with a quick gesture.

"Nothing, now," I answered, and we entered there.

Vialle turned her head in our direction as we came in, her expression as unreadable as Luke's.

"I take it you are properly attired now?" she asked.

"I am indeed," he answered.

"Then let's be about this," she said, raising her left hand, which I saw to contain a Trump. "Come over here, please."

Luke approached her and I followed him. I could see then that it was Julian's Trump that she held.

"Place your hand upon my shoulder," she told him.

"All right."

He did, and she reached, found Julian and began

speaking to him. Shortly, Luke was party to the conversation, explaining what he intended to do. I overheard Vialle saying that the plan had her approval.

Moments later I saw Luke raise his free hand and extend it. I also saw the shadowy figure of Julian reaching forward, though I was not part of the Trump nexus. This was because I had summoned my Logrus Sight and had become sensitive to such things. I needed it for the timing, not wanting Luke whisked away before I could move.

I let my hand fall upon his shoulder and I moved forward as he did.

"Merlin! What are you doing?" I heard Vialle call.

"I'd like to see what happens," I said. "I'll come right home when things are concluded," and the rainbow gate closed behind me.

We stood within the flickering light of oil lamps inside a large tent. From outside, I could hear the wind and the sounds of stirring branches. Julian stood facing us. He let Luke's hand fall and regarded him without expression.

"So you are Caine's killer," he said.

"I am," Luke replied.

And I was remembering that Caine and Julian had always been particularly close. If Julian were to kill Luke and cry vendetta, I was certain that Random would merely nod and agree. Perhaps he'd even smile. Hard to say. If I were Random, I would greet Luke's removal with a sigh of relief. In fact, that was one of the reasons I'd come along. Supposing this whole deal were a setup? I couldn't picture Vialle as a part of it, but she could easily have been deceived by Julian and Benedict. Supposing Dalt wasn't even out there?

Or suppose he were—and that what he'd really asked for was Luke's head? After all, he had tried to kill Luke fairly recently. I had to admit the possibility now, and I also had to admit that Julian was the most likely candidate to be a willing party to such a design. For the good of Amber.

Julian's gaze met mine, and I wore as affectless a mask as his own.

"Good evening, Merlin," he said. "Do you have a special part in this plan?"

"I'm an observer," I answered. "Anything else I may do will be dictated by circumstance."

From somewhere outside I heard the growling of a hellhound.

"So long as you keep out of the way," Julian said.

I smiled.

"Sorcerers have special ways of avoiding notice," I replied.

He studied me again, wondering, I am certain, whether that involved some sort of threat—to defend Luke or to avenge him.

Then he shrugged and turned away to where a small table held an unrolled map, weighted in place with a rock and a dagger. He indicated that Luke should join him there, and I followed when he did.

It was a map of the western fringe of Arden, and he pointed out our position on it. Garnath lay to our south-southwest, Amber to the southeast.

"Our troops are situated here," he said, with a movement of his finger. "And Dalt's are here." He described another line, roughly paralleling our own.

"What about Benedict's force?" I inquired.

He glanced at me, showing the slightest of frowns.

"It is good for Luke to know that there is such a force," he stated, "but not its size, location, or objective. That way, if Dalt were to capture and question him, he'd have a lot to worry about and nothing to act upon."

Luke nodded. "Good idea," he said.

Julian pointed again, to a spot midway between the lines. "This is the place where I met with him when we spoke earlier," he explained. "It is a clear, level area, in view of both sides during daylight. I'd suggest we use it again, for your meeting."

"All right," Luke said, and I noticed that as he spoke,

Julian's fingertips caressed the handle of the dagger that lay before him. Then I saw that Luke's right hand, in casual movement, had come to rest upon his belt, slightly to the left and near to his own dagger.

Simultaneously, then, Luke and Julian smiled at each other, and held it several seconds too long. Luke was bigger than Julian, and I knew he was fast and strong. But Julian had centuries of experience with weapons behind him. I wondered how I would intervene if either made a move toward the other, because I knew that I would try to stop them. But they let their hands fall to their sides then, as if by sudden agreement, and Julian said, "Let me offer you a glass of wine."

"Don't mind if I do," Luke replied, and I wondered whether my presence had kept them from fighting. Probably not. I'd the feeling that Julian had just wanted to make his feelings clear, and Luke had wanted to let him know he didn't give a damn. I really don't know which one I'd have bet on.

Julian placed three cups upon the table, filled them with Bayle's Best, gestured for us to help ourselves as he corked the bottle, then picked up the remaining cup and took a swallow before either of us could do more than sniff ours. A quick assurance that we weren't being poisoned and that he wanted to talk business.

"When I met with him we each brought two retainers along," he said.

"Armed?" I asked.

He nodded.

"More for show, really."

"Were you mounted or on foot?" Luke asked.

"On foot," he replied. "We each left our lines at the same time and proceeded at the same pace till we met there in the middle, several hundred paces from either side."

"I see," Luke said. "No hitches?"

"None. We talked and returned."

"When was this?"

"Around sundown."

"Did he seem to be a man in a normal state of mind?"

"I'd say. I count a certain arrogant posturing and a few insults toward Amber as normal for Dalt."

"Understandable," Luke said. "And he wanted me or my mother, or both? And failing to get us, he threatened to attack?"

"Yes."

"Did he give any indication as to why he wants us?"

"None," Julian replied.

Luke took a sip of his wine.

"Did he specify whether he wanted us dead or alive?" he asked.

"Yes. He wants you alive," Julian answered.

"What are your impressions?"

"If I give you to him, I'm rid of you," Julian said. "If I spit in his eye and take him on in battle, I'm rid of him. Either way, I come out ahead. . . ."

Then his gaze moved to the wine cup, which Luke had picked up with his left hand, and for an instant his eyes widened. I realized he had just then noticed that Luke was wearing Vialle's ring.

"It looks as if I get to kill Dalt, anyway," he concluded.

"By impressions," Luke went on, unperturbed, "I meant, do you believe he will really attack? Do you have any idea where he came from? Any indication where he might be headed when he leaves here—if he leaves?"

Julian swirled his wine in his cup.

"I have to go under the assumption that he means what he says and plans to attack. When we first became aware of his troop movements, he was advancing from the general direction of Begma and Kashfa—probably Eregnor, since he hangs out there a lot. Your guess is as good as anyone's as to where he wants to go if he leaves here."

Luke took a quick swallow of wine a fraction of a second too late for it to conceal what appeared to be a sudden smile. No, I realized right then, Luke's guess was not as good as anyone else's. It was probably a hell of a lot better. I took a quick drink myself, though I'm not sure what expression I might have been concealing.

"You can sleep here," Julian said. "If you're hungry, I'll have some food brought in. We'll set up this meeting for you at daybreak."

Luke shook his head.

"Now," Luke said, with another subtle but obvious display of the ring. "We want it set up right away."

Julian studied him for several pulsebeats. Then, "You'll not be in the clearest sight of either side in the dark, especially with snow coming down," he said. "Some little misunderstanding could result in an attack, from either side."

"If both of my companions bore large torches—and if both of his did the same—" he suggested, "we ought to be visible to both sides at a few hundred yards."

"Possibly," Julian said. "All right. I'll have the message sent to his camp, and I'll choose two retainers to accompany you."

"I already know who I want to have with me," Luke said. "Yourself and Merlin here."

"You are a curious individual," Julian observed. "But yes, I agree. I would like to be there when whatever happens, happens."

Julian moved to the front of his tent, opened the flap, and summoned an officer with whom he spoke for several minutes. In this space, I asked, "You know what you're doing, Luke?"

"Certainly," he replied.

"I've a feeling this is a little more than playing it by ear," I said. "Any reason why you can't tell me your plan?"

He appraised me for a moment, then said, "I only recently realized that I, too, am a son of Amber. We've met, and we've seen that we're too much like each other. Okay. That's good. It means we can do business, right?"

I allowed myself to frown. I wasn't sure what he was trying to say.

He clasped my shoulder lightly.

"Don't worry," he said. "You can trust me. Not that you have a great deal of choice at this point. But you may a bit later. I want you to remember then that, whatever happens, you must not interfere."

"What do you think is going to happen?"

"We haven't the time or the privacy to speculate," he said. "So let it go, and remember everything I said this evening."

"As you said, I haven't much choice at this point."

"I want you to remember it later," he said, as Julian lowered the flap and turned toward us.

"I'll take you up on that meal," Luke called to him. "How about you, Merle? Hungry?"

"Lord, no!" I replied. "I just sat through a state dinner."

"Oh?" he inquired almost too casually. "What was the occasion?"

I began to laugh. It was too much for one day. I was about to tell him that we hadn't the time or the privacy. But Julian had just reopened the tent flap and was calling for an orderly, and I wanted to throw a few curve balls through Luke's broken field just to see what they did to his composure.

"Oh, it was for the Begman prime minister, Orkuz, and some of his staff," I explained.

He waited while I pretended to take a long drink of wine. Then I lowered it and said, "That's all."

"Come on, Merlin. What's it about? I've been relatively square with you recently."

"Oh?" I said.

For a minute I didn't think he'd see the humor in it, but then he began to laugh, too.

"Sometimes the mills of the gods grind too damned fast and we get buried in grist," he observed. "Look, how about giving me this one for free. I don't have anything brief to trade right now. What's he want?''

"You'll bear in mind that this is classified until tomorrow?"

"Okay. What happens tomorrow?"

"Arkans, Duke of Shadburne, gets crowned in Kashfa."

"Holy shit!" Luke said. He glanced at Julian, then back at me. "That was a damned clever choice on Random's part," he said after a time. "I didn't think he'd move this fast."

He stared off into some vanishing point for a long while. Then he said, "Thanks."

"Well, does it help or hurt?" I asked.

"Me, or Kashfa?" he said.

"I hadn't split it down that fine."

"That's okay, because I'm not sure how to take this. I need to do some thinking. Get the big picture."

I stared at him and he smiled again.

"It *is* interesting," he added. "You got anything else for me?"

"That's enough," I said.

"Yeah, probably you're right," he agreed. "Don't want to overload the systems. Think we're losing touch with the simple things, old buddy?"

"Not so long as we know each other," I said.

Julian dropped the flap, returned to us, and sought his wine cup.

"Your food will be along in a few minutes," he told Luke.

"Thanks."

"According to Benedict," he said, "you told Random that Dalt is a son of Oberon."

"I did," Luke acknowledged. "One who's walked the Pattern, at that. Does it make a difference?"

Julian shrugged.

"Won't be the first time I've wanted to kill a relative," he stated. "By the way, you're my nephew, aren't you?"

"Right . . . uncle."

Julian swirled the contents of his cup again.

"Well, welcome to Amber," he said. "I heard a banshee last night. I wonder if there's any connection?"

"Change," Luke said. "They mean things are changing and they wail for what's being lost."

"Death. They mean death, don't they?"

"Not always. Sometimes they just show up at turning points for dramatic effect."

"Too bad," Julian said. "But one can always hope."

I thought Luke was going to say something else, but Julian began again before he could.

"How well did you know your father?" he asked.

Luke stiffened slightly, but answered, "Maybe not as well as most. I don't know. He was like a salesman. Always coming and going. Didn't usually stay with us long."

Julian nodded.

"What was he like, near the end?" he inquired.

Luke studied his hands.

"Well, he wasn't exactly normal, if that's what you mean," he finally said. "Like I was telling Merlin earlier, I think the process he undertook to gain his powers might have unbalanced him some."

"I never heard that story."

Luke shrugged.

"The details aren't all that important—just the results."

"You're saying he wasn't a bad father before that?"

"Hell, I don't know. I never had another father to compare him to. Why do you ask?"

"Curiosity. It's a part of his life I knew nothing about."

"Well, what kind of brother was he?"

"Wild," Julian said. "We didn't get along all that well. So we pretty much stayed out of each other's ways. He was smart, though. Talented, too. Had a flare for the arts. I was just trying to figure how much you might take after him."

Luke turned his hands palms upward.

"Beats me," he said.

"Well, no matter," Julian replied, setting down his cup and turning toward the front of the tent again. "I believe your food is about to arrive."

He moved off in that direction. I could hear the tiny crystals of ice rattling against the canvas overhead, and a few growls from outside: concerto for wind and hellhound. No banshees, though. Not yet.

CHAPTER 9

I walked a pace or so behind Luke, a couple of yards off to his left, trying to keep even with Julian, who was over to the right. The torch I bore was a big thing, about six tapering feet of pitchy wood, sharpened at its terminus to make it easy to drive into the ground. I held it at arm's distance, because the oily flames licked and lashed in all directions in accord with vagaries of the wind. Sharp, icy flakes fell upon my cheek, my forehead, my hands, with a few catching in my eyebrows and lashes. I blinked vigorously as the heat of the torch melted them and they ran into my eyes. The grasses beneath my feet were sufficiently cold to give a brittle, crunching sensation every time I took a step. Directly ahead I could see the slow advance of two other torches toward us, and the shadowy figure of a man who walked between them. I blinked and waited for the flow from one or the other of his torches to give me a better look. I'd only seen him once, very briefly, via Trump, back at Arbor House. His hair looked golden, or even coppery, by what light there was upon it; but I remembered it as a kind of dirty blond by natural light. His eyes, I recalled, were green, though there was no way I could see that now. I did begin to realize for the first time, however, that he was pretty big—either that or he had chosen fairly short torchbearers. He had been alone that one time I'd seen him, and I had had no standard for comparison. As the light from our torches reached him I saw that he had on a heavy, green sleeveless doublet without a collar, over something black and also heavy, with sleeves that extended down his arms to vanish within green gauntlets. His trousers were black, as were the high boots they entered; his cloak was black and lined with an emerald green that caught our light as the cloak furled about him in shifting, oily landscapes of yellow and red. He wore a heavy circular medallion, which looked to be gold, on a chain about his neck; and though I could not make out the details of its device, I was certain that it bore a Lion rending a Unicorn. He came to a halt about ten or twelve paces from Luke, who stopped an instant later. Dalt gestured, and his retainers drove the butts of their torches into the ground. Julian and I immediately did the same, and we remained near them, as Dalt's men were doing. Then Dalt nodded to Luke, and they both advanced again, meeting at the center of the box formed by the lights, clasping right forearms, staring into each other's eyes. Luke's back was to me, but I could see Dalt's face. He showed no signs of emotion, but his lips were already moving. I couldn't hear a word that was being said, between the wind and the fact that they seemed intentionally to be keeping it low. At least, I finally had a point of reference for Dalt's size. Luke is about six three, and I could see that Dalt was several inches taller. I glanced at Julian, but he was not looking my way. I wondered how many eyes regarded us from both sides of the field.

Julian is always a bad person to check for reactions. He was simply watching the two of them, expressionless, stolid. I cultivated the same attitude, and the minutes passed, the snow kept falling.

After a long while Luke turned away and headed back toward us. Dalt moved off toward one of his torch-bearers. Luke stopped midway between us, and Julian and I moved to join him.

"What's up?" I asked him.

"Oh," he said, "I think I found a way of settling this without a war."

"Great," I said. "What did you sell him?"

"I sold him on the idea of fighting a duel with me to determine how this thing goes," he explained.

"God damn it, Luke!" I said. "That guy's a pro! And I'm sure he's got our genetic package for strength. And he's been living in the field all this time. He's probably in top shape. And he outweighs you and outreaches you."

Luke grinned.

"So, I might get lucky," he said. He looked at Julian. "Anyway, if you can get a message back to the lines and tell them not to attack when we start this thing, Dalt's side will be holding still for it, too."

Julian looked over to where one of Dalt's torchbearers had started back toward his lines. He turned toward his own side then and executed a number of hand signals. Shortly, a man emerged from cover and began jogging toward us.

"Luke," I said. "This is crazy. The only way you're going to win is to get Benedict for a second and then break a leg."

"Merle," he said, "let it go. This is between Dalt and me. Okay?"

"I've got a bunch of fairly fresh spells," I said. "We can let this thing start, and then I'll hit him with one at the right time. It'll look as if you did it."

"No!" he said. "This really is a matter of honor. So you've got to stay out of it."

"Okay," I said, "if that's how you want it."

"Besides, nobody's going to die," he explained. "Neither of us wants that right now, and it's part of the deal. We're too valuable to each other alive. No weapons. Strictly *mano a mano*."

"Just what," Julian inquired, "*is* the deal?"

"If Dalt whips my ass," Luke replied, "I'm his prisoner. He'll withdraw his force and I'll accompany him."

"Luke, you're crazy!" I said.

Julian glared at me.

"Continue," he said.

"If I win, he's my prisoner," he went on. "He goes back with me to Amber, or anywhere else I care to transport him, and his officers withdraw his troops.'"

"The only way of assuring such a withdrawal," Julian said, "is to let them know that if they don't they're doomed."

"Of course," Luke said. "That's why I told him that Benedict is waiting in the wings to roll down on him. I'm sure it's the only reason he's agreed to do this."

"Most astute," Julian observed. "Either way, Amber wins. What are you trying to buy with this, Rinaldo, for yourself?"

Luke smiled.

"Think about it," he said.

"There is more to you than I'd thought, Nephew," he replied. "Move over there to my right, would you?"

"Why?"

"To block his view of me, of course. I've got to let Benedict know what's going on."

Luke moved while Julian located his Trumps and shuffled out the proper one. In the meantime the runner from our lines had come up and stood waiting. Julian put away all of the cards but one then, and commenced his communication. It lasted for a minute or so, then Julian paused to speak with the runner and send him back. Immediately, he continued the conversation with the card. When he finally stopped talking or seeming to listen, he did not restore the Trump to the inner pocket where he kept the others, but retained it in his hand out of sight. I realized then that the contact would not be broken, that he would stay in touch with Benedict until this business was finished, so that Benedict would know in an instant what it was that he must do.

Luke unfastened the cloak I'd lent him, came over, and handed it to me.

"Hold this till I'm done, will you?" he said.

"Yes," I agreed, accepting it. "Good luck."

He smiled briefly and turned away. Dalt was already moving toward the center of the square.

Luke advanced, also. He and Dalt both halted, facing each other, while there were still several paces separating them. Dalt said something I could not hear, and Luke's reply was lost to me, also.

Then they raised their arms. Luke struck a boxer's stance, and Dalt's hands came up in a wrestler's defense. Luke threw the first punch—or maybe it was just a feint; either way, it didn't land—toward Dalt's face. Dalt brushed at it and stepped back, and Luke moved in quickly and landed two blows on his midsection. Another shot at his face was blocked, though, and Luke began to circle, jabbing. Dalt tried rushing twice then and got clipped both times, a little trickle of blood coming from his lip after the second one. On his third rush, though, he sent Luke sprawling but was unable to crash down on top of him, as Luke was able to twist partly away and roll when he hit. He tried kicking Dalt in the right kidney, though, as soon as he'd scrambled to his feet, and Dalt caught his ankle and rose, bearing him over backward. Luke landed a kick on the side of his knee with his other foot as he went down, but Dalt kept hold of the foot, bearing down and beginning to twist. Luke bent forward then, grimacing, and managed to catch Dalt's right wrist with both hands and tear his foot free of the larger man's grip. He doubled and moved forward then, still holding the wrist, regaining his feet and straightening as he advanced, passing under Dalt's arm on his right side, turning, and dragging him face downward to the ground. He moved quickly then, bending the arm up into a hammerlock, holding it with his right hand and seizing a handful of Dalt's hair with his left. But as he drew Dalt's head backward—preparatory, I was certain, to slamming it a few times against the ground—I saw that it wasn't going to work. Dalt stiffened, and his arm started to move downward. He was straightening it against Luke's lock. Luke tried pushing Dalt's head forward several times then, without effect. It became apparent that if he released either hand he was in trouble, and he wasn't able to maintain the hold. Dalt was just too damned strong. Seeing this, Luke threw all of his weight against Dalt's back, pushed, and sprang up. He wasn't quite fast enough, however, because Dalt's freed arm swung around and clipped him across the left calf as he moved away. Luke stumbled. Dalt was up and swinging immediately. He caught Luke with a wild haymaker that knocked him over backward. This time, when he threw himself upon Luke, Luke was unable to roll free; he only managed to turn his body partly. Dalt landed with considerable force, twisting past a slow knee aimed toward his groin. Luke did not get his hands free in time to defend against a punch that caught him on the left side of the jaw. He turned with it and fell completely flat. Then his right hand snapped upward, its heel striking the point of Dalt's chin, fingers hooking toward the eyes. Dalt jerked his head back and slapped the hand away. Luke threw a hammer blow toward his temple with the other hand, and though it connected, Dalt was already moving his head to the side, and I couldn't see that it had any effect. Luke dropped both elbows to the ground and pushed himself up and forward, bowing. His forehead struck Dalt's face— where, I am not precisely certain—before he fell back. Moments later, Dalt's nose began bleeding as he reached out with his left hand to grasp Luke by the neck. His right hand, open, slapped Luke hard on the side of the head. I saw Luke's teeth just before it landed, as he tried biting at the incoming hand, but the grip on his neck prevented this. Dalt moved to repeat the blow, but this time Luke's left arm came up and blocked it, while his right hand caught hold of Dalt's left wrist in an effort to pull it away from his neck. Dalt's right hand snaked in past Luke's left then, to take hold, creating a two-handed grip on Luke's neck, thumbs moving to depress the windpipe.

I thought that might well be it. But Luke's right hand suddenly moved to Dalt's left elbow, his left hand crossed

both of Dalt's arms to seize the left forearm, and Luke
twisted his body and cranked the elbow skyward. Dalt
went over to the left and Luke rolled to the right and
regained his footing, shaking his head as he did so. This
time he did not try kicking Dalt, who was already
recovering. Dalt again extended his arms, Luke raised his
fists, and they began circling once more.

The snow continued to fall, the wind to slacken and
surge, sometimes driving the icy flakes hard against faces,
other times permitting the snow to descend like a troubled
curtain. I thought of all the troops about me and wondered
for a moment whether I would find myself in the middle
of a battlefield when this thing was finally over. The fact
that Benedict was ready to swoop down from somewhere
and wreak extra havoc did not exactly comfort me, even
though it meant that my side would probably win. I
remembered then that my being there was my own choice.

"Come on, Luke!" I yelled. "Flatten him!"

This produced a very odd effect. Immediately, Dalt's
torchbearers began shouting encouragement to him. Our
voices must have carried through the wind's lulls, for
shortly there came waves of sound, which I at first took
to be some distant part of the storm and only later realized
to be shouting coming from both lines. Only Julian
remained silent, inscrutable.

Luke continued to circle Dalt, throwing jabs and trying
occasional combinations, and Dalt kept swatting away at
them and trying to catch an arm. Both of them had blood
on their faces and both seemed a bit slower than they had
been earlier. I'd a feeling they'd both been hurt, though
it was impossible to guess to what extent. Luke had
opened a small cut high on Dalt's left cheek. Both of their
faces were beginning to look puffy.

Luke connected with another body combination, but it
was hard to say how much force there was behind the
blows. Dalt took them stoically and found extra energy
somewhere to rush forward and attempt to grapple. Luke
was slow in withdrawing and Dalt managed to draw him

into a clinch. Both tried kneeing the other; both turned their hips and avoided it. They kept tangling arms and twisting as Dalt continued reaching after a better grip and Luke kept defeating the efforts while attempting to free an arm and get in a punch. Both tried several forehead bashes and instep stompings, but all of these were avoided by the other. Finally, Luke succeeded in hooking Dalt's leg, driving him backward to the ground.

Half kneeling atop him then, Luke caught him with a left cross and followed it immediately with a right. He tried for another left then, and Dalt caught his fist, surged upward and threw him back to the ground. As Dalt hurled himself upon him again, his face a half mask of blood and dirt, Luke was somehow able to strike him beneath the heart, but this did not stop Dalt's right fist which came down like a falling rock on the side of Luke's jaw. Dalt followed it with a weak left to the other side, a weak right, paused to suck in a great breath, then landed a solid left. Luke's head rolled to the side and he did not move.

Dalt crouched there atop him, panting like a dog, studying his face as if suspecting some trick, his right hand twitching as if he were contemplating striking again.

But nothing happened. They remained in that position for ten or fifteen seconds before Dalt slowly drew himself erect, eased off of Luke to Luke's left, then rose carefully to his feet, swayed for a second and straightened fully.

I could almost taste the death spell I had hung earlier. It would only take a few seconds to nail him, and no one would be certain how he had died. But I wondered what would happen if he were to collapse now, too. Would both sides attack? It was neither this nor humanitarian considerations that finally restrained me, however. Instead, it was Luke's words, ''This really is a matter of honor. So you've got to stay out of it,'' and, ''Nobody's going to die. . . . We're too valuable to each other alive.''

Okay. There was still no sound of trumpets. No rush of men to combat. It seemed that things might actually go as had been agreed. This was the way Luke had wanted it. I was not going to interfere.

I watched as Dalt knelt and began to raise Luke from the ground. Immediately, he lowered him, then called to his two torchmen to come and carry him. Dalt rose again and faced Julian as the men advanced.

"I call upon you to observe the rest of our agreement," he said loudly.

Julian inclined his head slightly.

"We will, provided you do," he answered. "Have your men out of here by daybreak."

"We leave now," Dalt replied, and he began to turn away.

"Dalt!" I called out.

He turned back and regarded me.

"My name is Merlin," I said. "We've met, though I don't know whether you remember."

He shook his head.

I raised my right arm and pronounced my most useless and at the same time flashiest spell. The ground erupted before him, showering him with dirt and gravel. He stepped back and wiped his face, then looked down into the rough trench that had appeared.

"That is your grave," I said, "If Luke's death comes of this."

He studied me again.

"Next time I'll remember you," he said, and he turned and followed the men who were carrying Luke back to his lines.

I looked over at Julian, who was watching me. He turned away and uprooted his torch. I did the same. I followed him back the way we had come.

Later, in his tent, Julian observed, "That solves one problem. Possibly two."

"Maybe," I said.

"It takes care of Dalt for the moment."

"I guess."

"Benedict tells me the man is already breaking camp."

"I don't think we've seen the last of him."

"If that's the best he can manage for an army these days, it won't matter."

"Don't you get the impression this was an impromptu mission?" I asked. "I'd guess he pulled his force together very fast. It makes me think he had a tight schedule."

"You may be right there. But he really gambled."

"And he won."

"Yes, he did. And you shouldn't have shown him your power, there at the end."

"Why not?"

"You'll have a wary enemy if you ever go after him."

"He needed warning."

"A man like that lives with risks. He calculates and he acts. However he figures you, he won't change his plans at this point. Besides, you haven't seen the last of Rinaldo either. He's the same way. Those two understand each other."

"You may be right."

"I am."

"If the fight had gone the other way, do you think his army would have stood for it?" I asked.

Julian shrugged. "He knew mine would if he won, because he knew I stood to gain by it. That was sufficient."

I nodded.

"Excuse me," he said. "I have to report this business to Vialle now. I assume you'll want to trump through when I've finished?"

"Yes."

He produced a card and set about the business. And I found myself wondering, not for the first time, just what it was that Vialle sensed when it came to a Trump contact. I always see the other person myself, and all of the others say that they do, too. But Vialle, as I understood it, had been blind from birth. I've always felt it would be impolite to ask her, and for that matter it's occurred to me that her answer probably wouldn't make much sense to a sighted person. I'll probably always wonder, though.

As Julian addressed her shadowy presence, I turned my mind to the future. I was going to have to do something about Mask and Jurt soon, and it looked now as if I'd be doing it without Luke. Did I really want to follow his advice and try to talk Jasra into an alliance against them? Would the benefits really be worth the risk? And if I didn't, how would I manage the thing? Maybe I should make my way back to that strange bar and see about renting the Jabberwock. Or the Vorpal Sword. Or both. Maybe—

I heard my name mentioned, and I drifted back to the present moment, present problems. Julian was explaining something to Vialle, but I knew there wasn't all that much to explain. So I got to my feet, stretched, and summoned the Logrus Sight.

I saw her ghostly form clearly when I directed my vision toward the area before Julian. She was in that same stiff chair where I had last seen her. I wondered whether she had remained there the entire while or had just returned. I hoped she'd had a chance to go back and eat that dessert I hadn't had a shot at.

Julian glanced at me, then, "If you're ready to go, she's ready to take you through," he said.

I crossed over and stood beside him, dropping the Logrus vision as I did so. I had decided it was not a good idea to bring the forces of the Logrus and the Pattern into too great a proximity. I reached out and touched the card, and Vialle's image sprang into full focus. A moment, and it was no longer an image.

"Anytime," she said, extending a hand.

I reached out and took hold of it gently.

"So long, Julian," I said, as I stepped forward.

He did not reply. Or if he did, I didn't catch it.

"I did not mean for things to go this way," she told me immediately, not releasing my hand.

"There was no way of foreseeing what happened," I said.

"Luke knew," she replied. "It makes sense now, doesn't it? Some of those little remarks he made? He planned the challenge all along."

"I guess so," I said.

"He's gambling on something. I wish I knew what."

"I can't help you on that," I answered. "He didn't say anything to me about it."

"But you will be the one with whom he will get in touch, eventually," she said. "I want to know immediately when you hear from him."

"All right," I agreed.

She released my hand.

"It would seem there is nothing more to say, for the moment."

"Well," I began, "there is another matter I think you ought to know about."

"Oh?"

"It concerns Coral's not being present at dinner this evening."

"Go on," she said.

"You are aware that we took a long walk about town today?"

"I am," she said.

"We wound up below," I continued, "in the chamber of the Pattern. She'd expressed a desire to see it."

"Many visitors do. It is pretty much a matter of judgment whether to take them. Often they lose interest, though, when they learn about the stairway."

"I did tell her about it," I said, "but it didn't discourage her. When she got there, she set foot upon the Pattern—"

"No!" she cried. "You should have watched her more closely! All that other trouble with Begma . . . and now this! Where is her body?"

"Good question," I responded. "I don't know. But she was alive the last time I saw her. You see, she claimed

Oberon was her father, and then she proceeded to walk the Pattern. When she'd finished, she had it transport her somewhere. Now, her sister—who is aware that we went off together—is concerned. She was pestering me through dinner as to where Coral might be.''

"What did you tell her?"

"I told her that I'd left her sister enjoying some of the beauties of the palace and that she might be a bit late to dinner. As things wore on, though, she seemed to grow more concerned and made me promise to search for her tonight if she didn't turn up. I didn't want to talk about what had really happened because I didn't want to go into the business of Coral's parentage.''

"Understandable," she replied. "Oh, my."

I waited, but she said nothing more. I continued to wait.

Finally, "I was not aware of the late king's affair in Begma," she said, "so it is difficult to assess the impact of this revelation. Did Coral give you any indication as to how long she intended to stay away? And for that matter, did you provide her with any means of return?"

"I gave her my Trump," I said, "but she hasn't been in touch. I got the impression she didn't intend to be away for too long, though."

"This could be serious," Vialle decided, "for reasons other than the obvious. How does Nayda strike you?"

"She seemed quite sensible," I said. "Also, I believe she rather likes me."

Vialle brooded a moment, then said, "If word of this gets to Orkuz, he could well get the impression that we are holding her hostage against his proper performance in any negotiations which might arise out of the situation in Kashfa."

"You're right. I hadn't thought of that."

"He will. People tend to think of such matters when dealing with us. So what we need to do is buy some time and try to turn her up before this begins looking suspicious."

"I understand," I said.

"Most likely, he will send to her quarters soon—if he hasn't already done so—to discover why she was not present at dinner. If he can be satisfied now, you will have the entire night in which to try to locate her."

"How?"

"You're the magician. You figure it out. In the meantime, you say that Nayda is sympathetic?"

"Very much so."

"Good. It seems to me that the best course of action then would be to attempt to enlist her aid. I trust you to be tactful and do this in the least distressing manner possible, of course—"

"Naturally—" I began.

"—because of her recent illness," she went on. "All we need to do now is give the second daughter a heart attack."

"Illness?" I inquired. "She hadn't mentioned anything about that."

"I'd imagine the memory is still distressing. She was apparently quite close to death until very recently, then rallied suddenly and insisted on accompanying her father on this mission. He's the one who told me about it."

"She seemed fine at dinner," I said lamely.

"Well, try to keep her that way. I want you to go to her immediately, tell her what happened as diplomatically as possible, and try to get her to cover for her sister while you search for her. There is, of course, the risk that she will not believe you and that she will go directly to Orkuz. Perhaps you might employ a spell to prevent this. But we have no other choice that I can see. Tell me whether I'm wrong."

"You're not wrong," I said.

"Then I suggest you be about it . . . and report back to me immediately if there are any problems, or any progress, no matter what the hour."

"I'm on my way," I said.

I departed the room in a hurry but shortly came to a

halt. It occurred to me that while I knew the general area of the palace in which the Begman party was quartered, I did not really know where Nayda's rooms were located. I did not want to go back and ask Vialle because it would make me look stupid for not having found out during dinner.

It took me the better part of ten minutes to turn up a member of the palace staff able to give me directions—along with a smirk—and then to follow them at a jog until I stood before Nayda's door.

I ran my hand through my hair, brushed off my trousers and jacket, wiped my boots on the backs of my pants legs, took a deep breath, smiled, exhaled, and knocked.

The door opened a few moments later. It was Nayda. She returned my smile and stepped aside.

"Come in," she said.

"I was expecting the maid," I told her as I entered. "You surprised me."

"Since I was expecting you, I sent her off to bed early," she replied.

She had changed into an outfit that looked like a gray sweat suit with a black sash. She also had on a pair of black slippers, and she had removed most of her makeup. Her hair was now drawn back severely and tied with a black ribbon. She gestured toward a couch, but I did not move to seat myself.

I clasped her shoulder lightly and stared into her eyes. She moved nearer.

"How are you feeling?" I asked.

"Find out," she said softly.

I could not even permit myself a sigh. Duty called. I slipped my arms around her, drew her to me, and kissed her. I held the pose for several seconds, then drew away, smiled again, and said, "You feel fine to me. Listen, there are some things I did not tell you—"

"Shall we sit down?" she said, taking my hand and leading me toward the couch.

Vialle had told me to be diplomatic, so I followed her.

Immediately, she continued our embrace and began to add refinements. Damn! And me constrained to rush her out to cover for Coral. If she would, I'd be happy to cover her afterward. Or any other interesting position Begmans might go in for. I'd better ask quickly, though, I decided. A couple of minutes more and it would be very undiplomatic to begin talking about her sister. Today was just a bad day when it came to timing.

"Before we get too involved here," I said, "I've got to ask a favor of you."

"Ask me anything," she said.

"I think there's going to be a delay in turning up your sister," I explained, "and I'd hate to worry your father. Do you know whether he's sent to her rooms yet, or been by them, to check on her?"

"I don't believe so. He strolled off with Gérard and Mr. Roth after dinner. I don't think he's returned to his apartment yet."

"Could you possibly find a way of giving him the impression that she hasn't strayed? Buy me some time to find out where she's off to?"

She looked amused.

"And those things you haven't told me . . . ?"

"I'll give you the whole story if you'll do this for me."

She traced my jawline with her index finger.

"All right," she said then. "We have a deal. Don't go away."

She rose, crossed the room, and passed out into the hall, leaving the door a few inches ajar. Why hadn't I had a nice normal affair since Julia? The last woman I'd made love to had actually been under the control of that strange body-shifting entity. Now . . . Now there was the faintest of shadows across the couch, as I realized that I'd rather be holding Coral than her sister. That was ridiculous. I'd only known her for half a day. . . .

There had simply been too much activity since my return. I was getting punchy. That had to be it.

When she returned she seated herself on the couch again, but this time with a couple of feet separating us. She seemed cheerful enough, though she made no move to resume our earlier occupation.

"It's taken care of," she said. "He will be misled, if he asks."

"Thanks," I told her.

"Now it's your turn," she stated. "Tell me things."

"All right," I began, and I launched into the story of Coral and the Pattern.

"No," she interrupted. "Start at the beginning, would you?"

"What do you mean?"

"Give me your whole day, from the time you left the palace together until you parted."

"That's silly," I protested.

"Humor me," she said. "You owe me one, remember?"

"Very well," I agreed, and I started again. I was able to skip over the bit about blasting the table in the cafe, but when I glossed over the business in the sea caves by saying that we'd looked around in them and found them pretty, she interrupted me.

"Stop," she said. "You're leaving something out. What occurred in the caves?"

"What makes you say that?" I asked.

"That is a secret I do not care to share just now," she explained. "Suffice it to say I have a means of spot-checking your veracity."

"It's not relevant," I said. "It will just confuse the issue. That's why I omitted it."

"You said you'd give me the whole afternoon."

"All right, lady," I agreed, and I did.

She bit her lip while I told her about Jurt and the zombies, and she licked idly at the beads of blood that appeared thereafter.

"What are you going to do about him?" she asked suddenly.

"That's my problem," I said then. "I promised you the afternoon, not my memoirs and survival plans."

"It's just that. . . . Remember, I offered to try to help you?"

"What do you mean? Do you think you can nail Jurt for me? I've got news for you: He's practically a candidate for godhood at the moment."

"What do you mean by 'godhood'?" she asked.

I shook my head.

"It would take most of the night to tell you this story properly, and we don't have the time, not if I'm going to start looking for Coral soon. Just let me finish with the business about the Pattern, will you?"

"Go ahead."

I did, and she showed no surprise whatsoever at the matter of her sister's paternity. I was going to question her as to her lack of reaction. Then I said, the hell with it. She's done what I wanted, and I did what I promised. She hasn't had a heart attack. And now it's time to go.

"That's it," I said, and I added, "Thanks."

I began to rise, and she moved quickly and was hugging me again.

I returned her embrace for a moment, then said, "I'd really better be going. Coral could be in danger."

"The hell with her," she said. "Stay with me. We have more important things to talk about."

I was surprised by her callousness, but I tried not to show it.

"I've a duty to her," I said, "and I've got to see to it now."

"All right," she said, sighing. "I'd better come along and give you a hand."

"How?" I asked.

"You'd be surprised," she told me, and she was on her feet and smiling a twisted smile.

I nodded, feeling that she was probably right.

CHAPTER 10

We hiked back along the hallway to my apartment. When I opened the door and summoned the lights, Nayda did a fast survey of the first room. She froze when she saw my coatrack.

"Queen Jasra!" she said.

"Yep. She had a disagreement with a sorcerer named Mask," I explained. "Guess who won?"

Nayda raised her left hand and moved it in a slow pattern—behind Jasra's neck and down her back, across her chest, then downward again. I did not recognize any of the movements she was performing.

"Don't tell me that you're a sorceress, too," I said. "It seems that everyone I run into these days has had some training in the Art."

"I am not a sorceress," she answered, "and I've had no such training. I have only one trick and it is not sorcery, but I use it for everything."

"And what is that trick?" I asked.

She ignored the question, then said, "My, she's certainly tightly bound. The key lies somewhere in the region of her solar plexus. Did you know that?"

"Yes," I replied. "I understand the spell fully."

"Why is she here?"

"Partly because I promised her son Rinaldo I'd rescue her from Mask, and partly as an assurance against his good behavior."

I pushed the door shut and secured it. When I turned back, she was facing me.

"Have you seen him recently?" she said in a conversational tone.

"Yes. Why?"

"Oh, no special reason."

"I thought we were trying to help each other," I said.

"I thought we were looking for my sister."

"It can wait another minute if you know something special about Rinaldo."

"I was just curious where he might be right now."

I turned away and moved to the chest where I keep art supplies. I removed the necessary items and took them to my drawing board. While I was about it, I said, "I don't know where he is."

I set up the piece of pasteboard, seated myself and closed my eyes, summoning a mental image of Coral, preliminary to beginning her sketch. Again, I half wondered whether the picture in my mind, along with the appropriate magical endorsement, would be sufficient for contact. But now was not the time to mess around being experimental. I opened my eyes and began to draw. I used the techniques I'd learned in the Courts, which are different yet similar to those employed in Amber. I was qualified to execute them in either fashion, but I'm faster with the style I learned first.

Nayda came over and stood near, watching, not asking whether I minded. As it was, I did not.

"When did you see him last?" she asked.

"Who?"

"Luke."

"This evening," I answered.

"Where?"

"He was here earlier."

"Is he here now?"

"No."

"Where did you last see him?"

"In the forest of Arden. Why?"

"It seems a strange place to part."

I was working on Coral's eyebrows.

"We parted under strange circumstances," I said.

A little more work about the eyes, a bit on the hair. . . .

"Strange? In what way?" she asked.

More color to the cheeks. . . .

"Never mind," I told her.

"All right," she said. "It's probably not that important."

I decided against rising to that bait, because I was suddenly getting something. As had occasionally happened in the past, my concentration on the Trump as I put the final touches to it was sufficiently intense to reach through and. . . .

"Coral!" I said, as the features moved, perspectives shifted.

"Merlin . . . ?" she answered. "I . . . I'm in trouble."

Oddly, there was no background whatever. Just blackness. I felt Nayda's hand upon my shoulder.

"Are you all right?" I asked.

"Yes. . . . It's dark here," she said. "Very dark."

Of course. One cannot manipulate Shadow in the absence of light. Or even see to use a Trump.

"That's where the Pattern sent you?" I asked.

"No," she answered.

"Take my hand," I said. "You can tell me about it afterward."

I extended my hand and she reached toward it.

"They—" she began.

And with a stinging flash the contact was broken. I felt Nayda stiffen beside me.

"What happened?" she asked.

"I don't know. We were suddenly blocked. I can't tell what forces were involved."

"What are you going to do?"

"Try again in a little bit," I said. "If it were a reaction

thing, resistance will probably be high just now, and it may ease up later. At least she says she's all right.''

I withdrew the packet of Trumps I normally carry, shuffled out Luke's. Now seemed as good a time as any to see how he was faring. Nayda glanced at the card and smiled.

''I thought you just saw him a little while ago,'' she said.

''A lot can happen in a little while.''

''I'm certain a lot *has* happened.''

''You think you know something about what's going on with him?'' I asked.

''Yes. I do.''

I raised the Trump.

''What?'' I said.

''I'd be willing to wager, you won't get through to him.''

''We'll see.''

I concentrated and I reached. I reached again. A minute or so later I wiped my brow.

''How'd you know?'' I asked.

''Luke's blocking you. I would, too . . . under the circumstances.''

''What circumstances?''

She gave me a quirked smile, crossed to a chair, and sat down.

''Now I have something to trade with you again,'' she said.

''Again?''

I studied her. Something jiggled and fell into place.

''You've been calling him 'Luke' rather than 'Rinaldo,' '' I said.

''So I have.''

''I'd been wondering when you'd show up again.''

She continued to smile.

''I went and shot my eviction-notice spell,'' I observed. ''Can't complain, though. It probably saved my life. Do I owe you that one, in some roundabout fashion?''

"I'm not proud. I'll take it."

"I'm going to ask you again what you want, and if you say it's to help me or to protect me, I'm going to turn you into a coatrack."

She laughed.

"I'd have guessed you'd take whatever help you could get right now," she said.

"A lot depends on what you mean by 'help.' "

"If you'll tell me what you have in mind, I'll tell you whether I can be of any assistance."

"All right," I said. "I'm going to change clothes while I talk, though. I don't feel like storming a citadel dressed like this. May I lend you something tougher than a sweat suit?"

"I'm fine. Start at Arbor House, okay?"

"Okay," I said, and I proceeded to fill her in while I garbed myself in tougher fare. She was no longer a pretty lady to me, but rather a nebulous entity in human form. She seated herself while I was talking and stared at the wall, or through it, over steepled fingers. When I was finished, she kept staring, and I went over to my drawing board, took up Coral's Trump, tried again, but couldn't get through. I tried Luke's card, also, with the same results.

As I was about to replace Luke's Trump, square the deck, and case it, I glimpsed the next lower card and a lightning chain of recollections and speculations flashed through my mind. I removed the card and focused on it. I reached. . . .

"Yes, Merlin?" he said moments later, seated at a small table on a terrace—evening skyline of a city behind him—lowering what appeared to be a cup of espresso to a tiny white saucer.

"Right now. Hurry," I said. "Come to me."

Nayda had begun to make a low growling sound just as the contact occurred, and she was on her feet and moving toward me, her eyes fixed upon the Trump, just as Mandor took my hand and stepped through. She halted when the tall, black-garbed figure appeared before her. They regarded each other without expression for a moment, and then she took a long sliding step toward him, her hands beginning to rise. Immediately, from the depth of some inner cloak pocket where his right hand was thrust, there came a single, sharp, metallic click.

Nayda froze.

"Interesting," Mandor said, raising his left hand and passing it in front of her face. Her eyes did not follow it. "This is the one you told me about earlier—Vinta, I believe, you called her?"

"Yes, only now she's Nayda."

He produced a small, dark metal ball from somewhere and held it upon the palm of his left hand, which he extended before her. Slowly, the ball began to move, describing a counterclockwise circle. Nayda emitted a single sound, something halfway between a cry and a gasp, and she dropped forward to her hands and knees, head lowered. From where I stood I could see saliva dripping from her mouth.

He said something very fast, in an archaic form of Thari which I could not follow. She responded in the affirmative.

"I believe I've solved your mystery," he said then. "Do you recall your lessons on Respondances and High Compellings?"

"Sort of," I said. "Academically. I was never exactly swept away by the subject."

"Unfortunate," he stated. "You should report back to Suhuy for a postgraduate course sometime."

"Are you trying to tell me . . . ?"

"The creature you see before you, inhabiting a not unattractive human form, is a *ty'iga*," he explained.

I stared. The *ty'iga* were a normally bodiless race of demons that dwelled in the blackness beyond the Rim. I recalled being told that they were very powerful and very difficult to control.

"Uh . . . can you make this one stop slobbering on my carpet?" I said.

"Of course," he replied, and he released the sphere, which fell to the floor before her. It did not bounce, but began immediately to roll, describing a rapid circuit about her.

"Stand up," he said, "and stop releasing bodily fluids upon the floor."

She did as he ordered, climbing to her feet, her expression vacant.

"Seat yourself in that chair," he directed, indicating the one she had occupied but minutes earlier.

She complied, and the rolling ball adjusted itself to her progress and continued its circle, about the chair now.

"It cannot vacate that body," he said then, "unless I release it. And I can cause it any amount of torment within my sphere of power. I can get you your answers now. Tell me what the questions are."

"Can she hear us right now?"

"Yes, but it cannot speak unless I permit it."

"Well, there's no point to causing unnecessary pain. The threat itself may be sufficient. I want to know why she's been following me about."

"Very well," he said. "That is the question, *ty'iga.* Answer it!"

"I follow him to protect him," she said, her voice flat.

"I've already heard that one," I said. "I want to know why."

"Why?" Mandor repeated.

"I must," she answered.

"Why must you?" he asked.

"I. . . ." Her teeth raked her lower lip and the blood began to flow again.

"Why?"

Her face grew flushed and beads of perspiration appeared upon her brow. Her eyes were still unfocused, but they brimmed with tears. A thin line of blood trickled down her chin. Mandor extended a clenched fist and opened it, revealing another metal ball. He held this one about ten inches before her brow, then released it. It hung in the air.

"Let the doors of pain be opened," he said, and he flicked it lightly with a fingertip.

Immediately, the small sphere began to move. It passed about her head in a slow ellipse, coming close to her temples on each orbit. She began to wail.

"Silence!" he said. "Suffer in silence!"

The tears ran down her cheeks, the blood ran down her chin. . . .

"Stop it!" I said.

"Very well." He reached over and squeezed the ball for a moment between the thumb and middle finger of his left hand. When he released it, it remained stationary, a small distance before her right ear. "Now you may answer the question," he said. "That was but the smallest sample of what I can do to you. I can push this to your total destruction."

She opened her mouth but no words came forth. Only a gagging sound.

"I think we may be going about this wrong," I said. "Can you just have her speak normally, rather than this question-and-answer business?"

"You heard him," Mandor said. "It is my will, also."

She gasped, then said, "My hands. . . . Please free them."

"Go ahead," I said.

"They are freed," Mandor stated.

She flexed her fingers.

"A handkerchief, a towel . . . ," she said softly.

I drew open a drawer in a nearby dresser, took out a handkerchief. As I moved to pass it to her, Mandor seized my wrist and took it from me. He tossed it to her and she caught it.

"Don't reach within my sphere," he told me.

"I wouldn't hurt him," she said, as she wiped her

eyes, her cheeks, her chin. "I told you, I mean only to protect him."

"We require more information than that," Mandor said, as he reached for the sphere again.

"Wait," I said. Then, to her, "Can you at least tell me why you can't tell me?"

"No," she answered. "It would amount to the same thing."

Suddenly I saw it as a strange sort of programming problem, and I decided to try a different tack.

"You must protect me at all costs?" I said. "That is your primary function?"

"Yes."

"And you are not supposed to tell me who set you this task, or why?"

"Yes."

"Supposing the only way you could protect me would be by telling me these things?"

Her brow furrowed.

"I . . . ," she said. "I don't. . . . The *only* way?"

She closed her eyes and raised her hands to her face.

"I. . . . Then I would have to tell you."

"Now we're getting somewhere," I said. "You would be willing to violate the secondary order in order to carry out the primary one?"

"Yes, but what you have described is not a real situation," she said.

"I see one that is," Mandor said suddenly. "You cannot follow that order if you cease to exist. Therefore, you would be violating it if you permit yourself to be destroyed. I will destroy you unless you answer those questions."

She smiled.

"I don't think so," she said.

"Why not?"

"Ask Merlin what the diplomatic situation would be if a daughter of the Begman prime minister were found dead in his room under mysterious circumstances—especially when he's already responsible for the disappearance of her sister."

Mandor frowned and looked at me.

"I don't understand what that's all about," he said.

"It doesn't matter," I told him. "She's lying. If something happens to her, the real Nayda simply returns. I saw it happen with George Hansen, Meg Devlin, and Vinta Bayle."

"That is what would normally occur," she said, "except for one thing. They were all alive when I took possession of their bodies. But Nayda had just died, following a severe illness. She was exactly what I needed, though, so I took possession and healed the body. She is not here anymore. If I depart, you'll be left either with a corpse or a human vegetable."

"You're bluffing," I said, but I remembered Vialle's saying that Nayda had been ill.

"No," she said. "I'm not."

"It doesn't matter," I told her.

"Mandor," I said, turning to him, "you said you can keep her from vacating that body and following me?"

"Yes," he replied.

"Okay, Nayda," I said. "I am going somewhere and I am going to be in extreme danger there. I am not going to permit you to follow me and carry out your orders."

"Don't," she answered.

"You give me no choice but to keep you pent while I go about my business."

She sighed.

"So you've found a way to get me to violate one order in order to get me to carry out the other. Very clever."

"Then you'll tell me what I want to know?"

She shook her head.

"I am physically unable to tell you," she said. "It is not a matter of will. But . . . I think I've found a way around it."

"What is that?"

"I believe I could confide in a third party who also desires your safety."

"You mean—"

"If you will leave the room for a time, I will try to tell your brother those things I may not explain to you."

My eyes met Mandor's. Then, "I'll step out in the hall for a bit," I said.

And I did. A lot of things bothered me as I studied a tapestry on the wall, not the least being that I had never told her that Mandor was my brother.

When my door opened after a long while, Mandor looked in both directions. He raised his hand when I began to move toward him. I halted, and he stepped outside and came toward me. He continued to glance about as he advanced.

"This is Amber palace?" he inquired.

"Yes. Not the most fashionable wing, perhaps, but I call it home."

"I'd like to see it under more relaxed circumstances," he said.

I nodded. "It's a date. So tell me, what happened in there?"

He looked away, discovered the tapestry, studied it.

"It's very peculiar," he said. "I can't."

"What do you mean?"

"You still trust me, don't you?"

"Of course."

"Then trust me in this. I've a good reason for not telling you what I learned."

"Come on, Mandor! What the hell's going on?"

"The *ty'iga* is not a danger to you. It really does care about your welfare."

"So what else is new? I want to know why."

"Leave it," he said, "for now. It's better that way."

I shook my head. I made a fist and looked around for something to hit.

"I know how you feel, but I'm asking you to drop it," he said.

"You mean the knowledge would hurt me in some way?"

"I didn't say that."

"Or do you mean that you're afraid to tell me?"

"Drop it!" he said.

I turned away and got control of myself.

"You must have a good reason," I finally decided.

"I do."

"I'm not going to give up on this," I told him. "But I haven't the time to pursue it further against this kind of resistance. Okay, you have your reasons and I have pressing business elsewhere."

"She mentioned Jurt and Mask and the Keep where Brand gained his powers," he said.

"Yes, that's where I'll be heading."

"She expects to accompany you."

"She is wrong."

"I would counsel against taking her, too."

"You'll keep her for me until I've taken care of things?"

"No," he said, "because I'm coming with you. I'll put her into a very deep trance, though, before we depart."

"But you don't know what's been going on since our dinner. A lot has happened, and I just haven't the time to bring you up to date."

"It doesn't matter," he said. "I know that it involves an unfriendly sorcerer, Jurt, and a dangerous place. That's enough. I'll come along and give you a hand."

"But that may not be enough," I countered. "*We* may not be enough."

"Even so, I think the *ty'iga* could turn into a hindrance."

"I wasn't referring to her. I was thinking about the stiff lady near the door."

"I'd meant to ask you about her. Some enemy you're punishing?"

"She had been an enemy, yes. And she's nasty, untrustworthy, and has a poisonous bite. She's also a deposed queen. I didn't freeze her, though. The sorcerer who's after me did it. She's the mother of a friend, and I rescued her and brought her back here for safekeeping. I had no reason for releasing her, until now."

"Ah, as an ally against her old enemy."

"Exactly. She's well acquainted with the place I'm going. But she doesn't like me and she's not easy to deal with—and I don't really know whether her son gave me enough ammunition to make her trustworthy."

"Do you feel she'd be a real asset?"

"Yes. I'd like to have all of that animus on my side. And I understand she's an accomplished sorceress."

"If additional persuading is needed, there are only threats and bribes. I've a few private hells I've designed and furnished—for purely esthetic reasons. She might find a quick tour very impressive. On the other hand, I could send for a pot of jewels."

"I don't know," I said. "Her motivations are somewhat complex. Let me handle this, as far as I'm able."

"Of course. Those were only suggestions."

"As I see it, the next order of business is to rouse her, put the proposition to her, and attempt to judge her response."

"There is no one else you might bring along, from among your kinsmen here?"

"I'm afraid to let any of them know I'm going. It could easily result in an order not to, until Random gets back. I haven't the time to wait around."

"I might summon some reinforcement from the Courts."

"Here? To Amber? I'd really be up shit creek if Random ever got wind of that. He might start suspecting subversion."

He smiled.

"This place reminds me a bit of home," he remarked, turning back toward my door.

When we entered, I saw that Nayda was still seated, her hands upon her knees, staring at a metal ball that hovered about a foot before her. The other continued its slow circuit down on the floor.

Seeing the direction of my gaze, Mandor remarked, "Very light trance state. She can hear us. You can rouse her in an instant if you wish."

I nodded and turned away. Now it was Jasra's turn.

I removed all of the garments I'd hung upon her and placed them on a chair across the room. Then I fetched a cloth and the basin and washed the clown makeup off her face.

"Am I forgetting anything?" I said, half to myself.

"A glass of water and a mirror," Mandor stated.

"What for?"

"She may be thirsty," he replied, "and I can just tell she'll want to look at herself."

"You may have a point there," I said, drawing up a small table. I placed a pitcher and a goblet upon it; also, a hand mirror.

"I'd also suggest you support her, in case she collapses when the spell is removed."

"True."

I placed my left arm about her shoulders, thought of her deadly bite, stepped back, and held her at arm's distance with the one hand.

"If she bites me, it will knock me out almost instantly," I said. "Be ready to defend yourself quickly if this occurs."

Mandor tossed another metal ball into the air. It hung there for an unnaturally long moment at the top of its arc, then dropped back to his hand.

"All right," I said, and then I spoke the words that raised the spell.

Nothing as dramatic as I'd feared ensued. She slumped and I supported her. "You're safe," I said, and added,

"Rinaldo knows you're here," to invoke the most familiar. "Here's a chair. Do you want some water?"

"Yes," she replied, and I poured some and passed it to her.

Her eyes were darting, taking in everything as she drank. I wondered whether she'd recovered instantly and might not now be stalling for time as she sipped, her mind racing, spells dancing at her fingertips. Her eyes returned more than once to Mandor, appraising, though she gave Nayda a long, hard stare.

Finally, she lowered the goblet and smiled.

"I take it, Merlin, that I am your prisoner," she said, choking slightly. She took another sip.

"Guest," I replied.

"Oh? How did this come about? Accepting the invitation escapes my mind."

"I brought you here from the citadel at the Keep of the Four Worlds in a somewhat cataleptic condition," I said.

"And where might 'here' be?"

"My apartment in the Palace of Amber."

"Prisoner, then," she stated.

"Guest," I repeated.

"In that case, I should be introduced, should I not?"

"Excuse me. Mandor, I introduce Her Highness Jasra, Queen of Kashfa." (I intentionally omitted the "Most Royal" part.) "Your Majesty, I request leave to present my brother, Lord Mandor."

She inclined her head, and Mandor approached, dropped to one knee, and raised her hand to his lips. He's better at such courtly gestures than I am, not even sniffing the back of her hand for the scent of bitter almonds. I could tell that she liked his manner—and she continued to study him afterward.

"I was not aware," she observed, "that the royal house here contained an individual named Mandor."

"Mandor is heir to the dukedom of Sawall in the Courts of Chaos," I replied.

Her eyes widened.

"And you say he is your brother?"

"Indeed."

"You've succeeded in surprising me," she stated. "I had forgotten your double lineage."

I smiled, nodded, stepped aside and gestured.

"And this—" I began.

"I am acquainted with Nayda," she said. "Why is the girl . . . preoccupied?"

"That represents a matter of great complexity," I said, "and there are other things I am certain you will find to be of much greater interest."

She cocked an eyebrow at me.

"Ah! That fragile, perishable item—the truth," she said. "When it surfaces so quickly there is usually a claustrophobia of circumstance. What is it that you want of me?"

I held my smile.

"It is good to appreciate circumstance," I said.

"I appreciate the fact that I am in Amber and alive and not occupying a cell, with two gentlemen behaving in a conciliatory fashion. I also appreciate the fact that I am not in the straits my most recent memories indicate I should occupy. And I have you to thank for my deliverance?"

"Yes."

"Somehow I doubt it was a matter of altruism on your part."

"I did it for Rinaldo. He tried getting you out once and got clobbered. Then I figured a way that might work, and I tried it. It did."

Her facial muscles tightened at the mention of her son's name. I'd decided she'd prefer hearing the one she'd given him, rather than "Luke."

"Is he all right?" she asked.

"Yes," I said, hoping it were so.

"Then why is he not present?"

"He's off somewhere with Dalt. I'm not sure as to his location. But—"

Nayda made a small noise just then, and we glanced her way. But she did not stir. Mandor gave me an inquiring look, but I shook my head slightly. I did not want her roused just then.

"Bad influence, that barbarian," Jasra observed, choking again and taking another drink. "I'd so wanted Rinaldo to acquire more of the courtly graces, rather than doing rude things on horseback much of the time," she continued, glancing at Mandor and granting him a small smile. "In this, I was disappointed. Do you have something stronger than water?"

"Yes," I replied, and I uncorked a bottle of wine and poured some into a goblet for her. I glanced at Mandor and at the bottle then, but he shook his head. "But you have to admit he did well in that track meet against UCLA, in his sophomore year," I said, not to let her put him down completely. "A certain amount of that comes from the more vigorous side of life."

She smiled as she accepted the drink.

"Yes. He broke a world record that day. I can still see him passing over the final hurdle."

"You were there?"

"Oh, yes. I attended all of your meets. I even watched you run," she said. "Not bad."

She sipped the wine.

"Would you like me to send for a meal for you?" I asked.

"No, I'm not really hungry. We were talking about truth a little while ago. . . ."

"So we were. I gather there had been some sorcerous exchange back at the Keep, between you and Mask—"

"Mask?" she said.

"The blue-masked sorcerer who rules there now."

"Oh, yes. Quite."

"I do have the story right, don't I?"

"Yes, but the encounter was more than a little traumatic. Forgive my hesitation. I was surprised and did not get my defenses up in time. That was really all there was to it. It will not happen again.''

"I'm sure. But—"

"Did you spirit me away?" she interrupted. "Or did you actually fight with Mask to get me free?"

"We fought," I said.

"In what condition did you leave Mask?"

"Buried under a pile of manure," I said.

She chuckled.

"Wonderful! I like a man with a sense of humor."

"I have to go back," I added.

"Oh? Why is that?"

"Because Mask is now allied with an enemy of mine— a man named Jurt, who desires my death."

She shrugged slightly.

"If Mask is no match for you, I fail to see where Mask and this man should represent a great problem."

Mandor cleared his throat.

"Begging your leave," he said. "But Jurt is a shape shifter and minor sorcerer from the Courts. He also has power over Shadow."

"I suppose that would make something of a differ- ence," she said.

"Not as much as what the two of them apparently plan to accomplish," I told her. "I believe that Mask intends running Jurt through the same ritual your late husband undertook—something involving the Fount of Power."

"No!" she cried, and she was on her feet, the rest of the wine mixing with Nayda's spittle and a few old bloodstains on the Tabriz I'd purchased for its delicately detailed pastoral scene. "It must not happen again!"

A storm came and went behind her eyes. Then, for the first time, she looked vulnerable.

"I lost him because of that . . . ," she said.

Then the moment was gone. The hardness returned.

"I had not finished my wine," she said then, reseating herself.

"I'll get you another glass," I told her.

"And is that a mirror on the table?"

CHAPTER 11

I waited till she was finished primping, glancing out of the window at the snow and surreptitiously trying again to reach Coral or Luke while my back was turned to her. No luck, though. When she put down the comb and brush she'd borrowed from me and laid the mirror beside them, I gathered she'd finished organizing her thoughts as well as her hair and was ready to talk again. I turned back slowly and strolled over.

We studied each other while practicing expressionlessness, then she asked, "Is anyone else in Amber aware that you have awakened me?"

"No," I replied.

"Good. That means I've a chance of leaving here alive. Presumably, you want my assistance against Mask and this Jurt?"

"Yes."

"Exactly what sort of help do you desire, and what are you prepared to pay for it?"

"I intend to penetrate the Keep and neutralize Mask and Jurt," I said.

" 'Neutralize'? That's one of those little euphemisms for 'kill,' isn't it?"

"I suppose so," I replied.

"Amber has never been noted for its squeamishness," she said. "You have been exposed to too much American journalism. So, you are aware of my familiarity with the

Keep, and you want my help in killing the two of them. Correct?''

I nodded.

"Rinaldo has told me that if we were to arrive too late and Jurt had already undergone the transformational ritual, you might know a way to use that same power against him," I explained.

"He'd gotten further into those notes than I'd realized," she said. "I am going to have to be frank with you then, since our lives may depend on it: Yes, there is such a technique. But no, it won't be of any help to us. Some preparations are required to turn the power to such an end. It is not something I could simply reach out and do at a moment's notice."

Mandor cleared his throat.

"I'd rather not see Jurt dead," he stated, "if there's a possibility I could take him back to the Courts as a prisoner. He could be disciplined. There might be a way of neutralizing him without really . . . neutralizing him, as you put it."

"And if there isn't?" I asked.

"Then I'll help you to kill him," he said. "I have no illusions about him, but I feel obliged to try something. I'm afraid that the news of his death could push our father over the edge."

I looked away. He could be right, and even though old Sawall's death would mean his own succession to the title and control of considerable holdings, I was certain he was not anxious to acquire them at that price."

"I understand," I said. "I hadn't thought of that."

"So give me a chance to subdue him. If I fail, I'll join you in whatever must be done."

"Agreed," I said, watching to see how Jasra was taking this.

She was studying us, a curious expression on her face.

" 'Our father'?" she said.

"Yes," I replied. "I wasn't going to mention that, but since it got out, Jurt's our younger brother."

Her eyes were alight now, at the scent of connivance.

"This is a family power struggle, isn't it?" she asked.

"I suppose you could put it that way," I said.

"Not really," Mandor said.

"And yours is an important family in the Courts?"

Mandor shrugged. So did I. I'd a feeling she was trying to figure a way to cash in on that end of it, too, and I decided to stonewall her.

"We were discussing the task at hand," I said. "I want to take us in there and accept Mask's challenge. We stop Jurt if he gets in the way and give him to Mandor. If it is impossible simply to subdue him, we go the rest of the way. Are you with us?"

"We have not yet discussed the price," she said.

"All right," I acknowledged. "I've talked about this with Rinaldo, and he told me to tell you that he's called the vendetta off. He feels things were settled with Amber when Caine died. He asked me to release you if you would go along with this, and he suggested that in return for your help against the new lord of the citadel we restore the Keep of the Four Worlds to your sovereignty. Bottom line, as he put it. What do you say?"

She picked up the goblet and took a long, slow sip. She'd stall, I knew, trying to figure a way to squeeze more out of this deal.

"You've spoken with Rinaldo very recently?" she said.

"Yes."

"I am not clear as to why he is running about with Dalt, rather than being here with us, if he is so much in agreement with this plan."

I sighed.

"Okay, I'll tell you the story," I said. "But if you're with us, I do want to get moving soon."

"Proceed," she said.

So I recounted the evening's adventure in Arden, omitting only the fact that Vialle had placed Luke under her protection. Nayda seemed to grow progressively distressed as I told the tale, uttering small whimpering sounds at odd intervals.

When I was finished, Jasra placed her hand upon Mandor's arm and rose, brushing him lightly with her hip as she passed, and she went to stand before Nayda.

"Now tell me why the daughter of a high Begman official is restrained here," she said.

"She is possessed of a demon that enjoys interfering in my affairs," I explained.

"Really? I've often wondered what hobbies demons might pursue," she observed. "But it seems this particular demon has been trying to say something in which I might be interested. If you would be so good as to free it for a moment's conversation I promise to consider your offer afterward."

"Time is running," I said.

"In that case my answer is no," she told me. "Lock me up someplace and go to the Keep without me."

I glanced at Mandor.

"In that I have not yet agreed to accept your offer," Jasra continued, "Rinaldo would call this an entertainment expense."

"I see no harm in it," Mandor said.

"Then let her speak," I told him.

"You may talk, *ty'iga,*" he said.

Her first words were not addressed to Jasra, however, but to me:

"Merlin, you have to let me accompany you."

I moved around to where I could see her face.

"No way," I told her.

"Why not?" she asked.

"Because your penchant for protecting me will actually hinder me in a situation where I will probably have to take some chances."

"That is my nature," she responded.

"And my problem," I said. "I mean you no ill. I'll be glad to talk to you when this is all over, but you're going to have to sit this one out."

Jasra cleared her throat.

"Is that the entire message? Or is there something you wished to tell me, also?" Jasra asked.

There followed a long silence, then, "Will you be accompanying them or not?" Nayda inquired.

Jasra took just as long to respond, obviously weighing her words:

"This is a clandestine, personal operation," she said. "I am not at all certain it would be countenanced by Merlin's seniors here in Amber. While it is true that I stand to gain if I cooperate, I will also undergo considerable risk. Of course, I want my freedom and the restoration of the Keep. It is almost a fair trade. But he also asks a quitclaim on the vendetta. What assurance have I that this means anything here, and that the hierarchy of Amber will not hunt me down as a troublemaker afterward? He cannot speak for the others when he operates on the sly this way."

Somehow, it had become a question addressed to me, and since it was a very good question to which I did not really have an answer, I was glad that the *ty'iga* had something to say:

"I believe that I can persuade you that it would be in your best interest to agree to accompany them and to render every assistance you can," she offered.

"Pray, begin," Jasra told her.

"I would have to speak with you in private on this matter."

Jasra smiled, out of her love for intrigue, I am certain.

"It is agreeable to me," she said.

"Mandor, force her to say it now," I said.

"Wait!" Jasra declared. "I will have this private conversation or you can forget about my help."

I began wondering just how much help Jasra really represented if she couldn't call upon the Fount to dispose of Jurt, should that become our biggest problem. True, she knew the Keep. But I didn't even know for certain how accomplished a sorceress she might be.

On the other hand, I wanted this thing settled now, and one more adept could make the difference.

"Nayda," I said, "are you planning something that could be damaging to Amber?"

"No," she replied.

"Mandor, what do *ty'iga* swear by?" I inquired.

"They don't," he said.

"What the hell," I said. "How much time do you want?"

"Give us ten minutes," she told me.

"Let's take a walk," I said to Mandor.

"Surely," he agreed, tossing another metal ball toward Nayda. It joined the others in orbit about her, a little above waist level.

I fetched a key from my desk drawer before departing. And as soon as we were in the hall I asked him, "Is there any way Jasra could free her?"

"Not with the additional circuit of confinement I established on the way out," he replied. "Not many could figure a way past it, and certainly not in ten minutes."

"She's just full of secrets, that damned *ty'iga*," I said. "Kind of makes me wonder who's really the prisoner here."

"She's only trading some bit of knowledge for Jasra's cooperation," he said. "She wants the lady to accompany us if she can't go herself, since it will mean extra protection for you."

"Then why can't we be present?"

"Nothing that I learned from her sheds any light on this," he said.

"Well, since I have a few minutes, there is a small errand I want to run. Would you keep an eye on things here and take charge if she calls us in before I get back?"

He smiled.

"If one of your relatives strolls by, should I introduce myself as a lord of Chaos?"

"I thought you were also a lord of deception."

"Of course," he said, and he clapped his hands and vanished.

"I'll hurry," I said.

"Cheerio," came his voice, from somewhere.

I hurried off up the hall. It was a little pilgrimage, I suppose—one that I had not made in a long while. On the brink of an enterprise such as this, it seemed somehow appropriate.

When I reached the door, I stood outside it for a moment, my eyes closed, visualizing the interior as last I had seen it. It was my father's apartment. I had wandered through it on many occasions, trying to judge from the furnishings, the layout, his bookshelves, and his curious collections something more than I already knew about the man. There was always some little thing that caught my attention, that answered a question or raised a new one—an inscription on the flyleaf of a book or a note in a margin, a silver hairbrush bearing the wrong set of initials, a daguerreotype of an attractive brunette signed "To Carl, Love, Carolyn," a snapshot of my father shaking hands with General MacArthur. . . .

I unlocked the door and pushed it open.

I did not move for several seconds, however, as a light glowed inside the place. For more long moments I listened, but there were no sounds from within. Slowly then, I entered. A number of candles burned upon the dresser set against the far wall. There was no one in sight.

"Hello?" I called out. "It's me. Merlin."

There came no answer.

I drew the door closed behind me and moved forward. A bud vase stood upon the dresser amid the candles. It contained a single rose, and it appeared to be silver in color. I drew nearer. Yes, it was real, not artificial. And it *was* silver. In what shadow did such flowers grow?

I picked up one of the candles by its holder and moved away with it, shielding its flame with my hand. I crossed to my left and entered the next room. Immediately, on opening the door, I saw that there was no need to have brought the candle. More of them were burning here.

"Hello?" I repeated.

Again, no answer. No sounds of any sort.

I set the candle upon a nearby table and crossed to the bed. I raised a sleeve and let it fall. A silvery shirt was laid out upon the counterpane beside a black pair of trousers—my father's colors. They had not been there when last I had visited.

I seated myself beside them and stared across the room into a shadowy corner. What was going on? Some bizarre household ritual? A haunting? or. . . .

"Corwin?" I said.

In that I'd hardly expected a reply, I was not disappointed. When I rose, however, I bumped against a heavy object hung upon the nearest bedpost. I reached out and raised it for a better view. A belt with a sheathed weapon hung upon it. These had not been present last time either. I gripped the haft and drew the blade.

A portion of the Pattern, contained within the gray metal, danced in the candlelight. This was Grayswandir, sword of my father. What it was doing back here now, I had no idea.

And I realized with a pang that I could not stick around to see what might be going on. I had to get back to my own problems. Yes, timing was definitely against me today.

I resheathed Grayswandir.

"Dad?" I said. "If you can hear me, I want to get together again. But I have to go now. Good luck on whatever you're about."

Then I departed the room, touched the silver rose as I passed and locked the door behind me. As I turned away, I realized that I was shaking.

I passed no one on the walk back, and when I approached my own door I wondered whether I should enter, knock, or wait. Then something touched my shoulder, and I turned around but no one was there. When

I turned forward once again Mandor stood before me, his brow slightly creased.

"What's the matter?" he asked. "You appear more troubled than when you left."

"Something totally different," I told him, "I think. Any word from inside yet?"

"I heard a shriek from Jasra while you were gone," he said, "and I hurried to the door and opened it. But she was laughing and she asked me to close it."

"Either *ty'igas* know some good stories or the news is favorable."

"So it would seem."

A little later the door opened and Jasra nodded to us.

"Our conversation is concluded," she said.

I studied her as I entered the room. She looked a lot more cheerful than she had seemed when we'd left. There was a bit more of a crinkling about the outer edges of her eyes, and she seemed almost to be fighting the corners of her mouth down into place.

"I hope it was a fruitful interview," I said.

"Yes. On the whole, I'd say it was that," she answered.

A glance at Nayda showed me that nothing had changed in terms of her position or expression.

"I'll have to be asking you for a decision now," I said. "I can't afford to cut things much closer than this."

"What happens if I say no?" she asked.

"I'll have you conducted to your quarters and inform the others that you're up and about," I said.

"As a guest?"

"As a very well-protected guest."

"I see. Well, I do not really care to inspect those quarters. I have decided to accompany you and assist you under the terms we discussed."

I bowed to her.

"Merlin!" Nayda said.

"No!" I answered, and I looked to Mandor.

He approached and stood before Nayda.

"It is best that you sleep now," he told her, and her eyes closed, her shoulders slumped. "Where is a good place for her to rest deeply?" he asked me.

"Through there," I said, indicating the doorway to the next room.

He took her by the hand and led her away. After a time, I heard him speaking softly, and then there was only silence. He emerged a little later, and I went to the door and glanced inside. She was stretched out on my bed. I did not see any of his metal spheres in the neighborhood.

"She's out of it?" I said.

"For a long time," he replied.

I looked at Jasra, who was glancing down into the mirror.

"Are you ready?" I inquired.

She regarded me through lowered lashes.

"How do you propose transporting us?" she asked.

"Do you have an especially tricky means of getting us in?"

"Not at the moment."

"Then I will be calling upon the Ghostwheel to take us there."

"Are you certain it is safe? I've conversed with that . . . device. I am not sure it is trustworthy."

"It's fine," I said. "Any spells you want to prime first?"

"Not necessary. My . . . resources should be in good order."

"Mandor?"

I heard a clicking sound from somewhere within his cloak.

"Ready," he said.

I withdrew the Ghostwheel Trump and studied it. I began my meditation. Then I reached. Nothing happened. I tried again, recalling, tuning, expanding. I reached again, calling, feeling. . . .

"The door . . . ," Jasra said.

I glanced at the door to the hallway, but there was

nothing unusual about it. Then I looked at her and realized the direction of her gaze.

The doorway to the next room, where Nayda slept, had begun to glow. It shone with a yellow light, and even as I watched, it grew in intensity. A spot of greater brightness then occurred at its center. Abruptly, the spot began a slow up-and-down movement.

Then came music, from where I was not certain, and Ghost's voice announced, "Follow the bouncing ball."

"Stop it!" I said. "It's distracting!"

The music went away. The circle of light grew still.

"Sorry," Ghost said. "I thought you'd find a little comic relief relaxing."

"You guessed wrong," I replied. "I just want you to take us to the citadel at the Keep of the Four Worlds."

"Do you want the troops, also? I can't seem to locate Luke."

"Just the three of us," I answered.

"What about the one who sleeps next door? I've met her before. She doesn't scan right."

"I know. She's not human. Let her sleep."

"Very well, then. Pass through the door."

"Come on," I said to the others, picking up my weapons belt and buckling it on, adding my spare dagger, grabbing my cloak off a chair, and drawing it over my shoulders.

I walked toward the portal and Mandor and Jasra followed. I stepped through, but the room was no longer there. Instead, there came a moment of blurring, and when my senses cleared, I was staring down and outward across a great distance beneath a heavily overcast sky, a cold wind whipping at my garments.

I heard an exclamation from Mandor and, a moment later, another from Jasra—behind me and to the left. The great ice field lay bone-white to my right, and in the opposite direction a slate-gray sea tossed whitecaps like serpents in a bucket of milk. Far below, before me, the dark ground simmered and steamed.

"Ghost!" I cried. "Where are you?"

"Here," came a soft response, and I looked down to behold a tiny ring of light near the toe of my left boot.

Directly ahead and below, the Keep stood stark in the distance. There were no signs of life outside its walls. I realized that I must be in the mountains, standing somewhere near the place where I had held my lengthy colloquy with the old hermit named Dave.

"I wanted you to take us into the citadel within the Keep," I explained. "Why did you bring us up here?"

"I told you I don't like that place," Ghost answered. "I wanted to give you a chance to look it over and decide exactly where you wished to be sent within. That way I can move very fast on the delivery, and not expose myself overlong to forces I find distressing."

I continued to study the Keep. A pair of twisters were again circling the outer walls. If there had not been a moat, they would probably have done a good job of creating one. They stayed almost exactly 180 degrees apart, and they took turns at illumination. The nearest one grew spark-shot with bolts of lightning, acquiring an eerie incandescence; then, as it began to fade, the other brightened. They passed through this cycle several times as I watched.

Jasra made a small noise, and I turned and asked her, "What's going on?"

"The ritual," she responded. "Someone is playing with those forces right now."

"Can you tell how far along they might be?" I asked.

"Not really. They could just be starting, or they could be finished already. All the poles of fire tell me is that everything is in place."

"You call it then, Jasra," I told her. "Where should we put in our appearance?"

"There are two long hallways leading to the chamber of the fountain," she said. "One is on the same level and the other a floor above it. The chamber itself is several stories high."

"I recall that," I acknowledged.

"If they are working directly with the forces and we simply appear within the chamber," she continued, "the advantage of surprise will only be momentary. I can't say for certain what they might hit us with. Better to approach along one of the two hallways and give me a chance to assess the situation. Since there is a possibility that they could note our approach along the lower hallway, the upper one would be best for all our purposes."

"All right," I agreed. "Ghost, can you put us back a distance in that upper hallway?"

The circle spread, tilted, rose, stood high above us for a moment, then dropped.

"You are . . . already . . . there," Ghost said, as my vision swam and the circle of light passed over us, head to toe. "Good-bye."

He was right. We were on target this time. We stood in a long, dim corridor, its walls of dark, hewn stone. Its one end was lost in darkness. Its other led into an area of illumination. The ceiling was of rough timbers, the heavy cross-beams softened by curtains and plumes of spider-webbing. A few blue wizard globes flickered within wall brackets, shedding a pale light that indicated they were near the ends of their spells. Others had already gone dead. Near the brighter end of the hallway some of these had been replaced by lanterns. From overhead came the sounds of small things scurrying within the ceiling. The place smelled damp, musty. But the air had an electric quality to it, as though we were breathing ozone, with an edge-of-event jitteriness permeating everything.

I shifted to Logrus Sight, and immediately there was a considerable brightening. Lines of force like glowing yellow cables ran everywhere. They provided the additional illumination I now perceived. And every time my movements intersected one, it heightened the overall tingling effect I experienced. I could see now that Jasra was standing at the intersection of several of these and seemed to be drawing energy from them into her body.

She was acquiring a glowing quality I was not certain my normal vision would have detected. When I glanced at Mandor I saw the Sign of the Logrus hovering before him also, which meant that he was aware of everything I was seeing.

Jasra began moving slowly along the corridor toward the lighted end. I fell in behind her and slightly to her left. Mandor followed me, moving so silently I had to glance back occasionally to assure myself he was still with us. As we advanced I became aware of a certain throbbing sensation, as of the beating of a vast pulse. Whether this was being transmitted through the floor or along those vibrating lines we continually encountered, I could not say.

I wondered whether our disturbing this net of forces was betraying our presence, and even our position, to the adept working with the stuff down at the Fount. Or was his concentration on the task at hand sufficiently distracting to permit us to approach undetected?

"It *has* started?" I whispered to Jasra.

"Yes," she replied.

"How far along?"

"The major phase could be completed."

A few paces more, and then she asked me, "What is your plan?"

"If you're right, we attack immediately. Perhaps we should try to take out Jurt first—all of us, I mean—if he's become that high-powered, that dangerous."

She licked her lips.

"I'm probably best equipped to deal with him, because of my connection with the Fount," she said then. "Better you don't get in my way. I'd rather see you dealing with Mask while I'm about it. It might be better to keep Mandor in reserve, to lend his aid to whichever of us might need it."

"I'll go along with your judgment," I said. "Mandor, did you hear all that?"

"Yes," he replied softly. "I'll do as she says."

Then, "What happens if I destroy the Fount itself?"
he asked Jasra.

"I don't believe it can be done," she answered.

He snorted, and I could see the dangerous lines along
which his thoughts were running.

"Humor me and suppose," he said.

She was silent for a time, then, "If you were able to
shut it down, even for a little while," she offered, "the
citadel would probably fall. I've been using its emana-
tions to help hold this place up. It's old, and I never got
around to buttressing it where it needs it. The amount of
energy required to attack the Fount successfully, though,
would be much better invested elsewhere."

"Thanks," he said.

She halted, extending a hand into one of the lines of
force and closing her eyes as if she were taking a pulse.

"Very strong," she said a little later. "Someone is
tapping it at deep levels now."

She began moving again. The light at the end of the
hallway grew brighter, then dimmer, brighter, dimmer.
The shadows retreated and flowed back repeatedly as this
occurred. I became aware of a sound something like the
humming of high wires. There was also an intermittent
crackling noise coming from that direction. I increased my
pace as Jasra began to hurry. At about that time there
came a sound of laughter from up ahead. Frakir tightened
upon my wrist. Flakes of fire flashed past the corridor's
mouth.

"Damn, damn, damn," I heard Jasra saying.

She raised her hand as we came into sight of the
landing where Mask had stood at the time of our
encounter. I halted as she moved very slowly,
approaching the railing. There were stairs both to the right
and the left, leading downward to opposite sides of the
chamber.

She looked down for only an instant; then she threw
herself back and to the right, rolling when she hit the
floor. Taking out a piece of railing, a ball of orange flame

fled upward like a slow comet, passing through the area she had just quitted. I rushed to her side, slipped an arm beneath her shoulders, began to raise her.

I felt her stiffen, as her head jerked slightly to the left. Somehow, I already knew what I would see when I turned that way.

Jurt stood there, stark naked save for his eye patch, glowing, smiling, a pulse away from substantiality.

"Good of you to drop by, brother," he said. "Sorry you can't stay."

Sparks danced at his fingertips as he swung his arm in my direction. I doubted that shaking hands was foremost in his mind.

The only response I could think of was, "Your shoelace is untied," which of course didn't stop him, but it actually had him looking puzzled for a second or two.

CHAPTER 12

Jurt had never played football. I do not believe he expected me to come up fast and rush him; and when it happened, I don't think he anticipated my coming in as low as I did.

And as for clipping him just above the knees and knocking him back through the opening in the railing, I'm sure he was surprised. At least he looked surprised as he went over backward and plummeted, sparks still dancing at his fingertips.

I heard Jasra chuckle, even as he faded in mid-fall and vanished before the floor got to spread him around a bit. Then, from the corner of my eye, I saw her rise.

"I'll deal with him now," she said, and, "No problem. He's clumsy," even as he appeared at the head of the stair to her right. "You take care of Mask!"

Mask was on the opposite side of the black stone fountain, staring up at me through an orange and red geyser of flames. Below, in the basin, the fires rippled yellow and white. When he scooped up a handful and worked them together as a child might shape a snowball, they became an incandescent blue. Then he threw it at me.

I sent it past with a simple parry. This was not Art, it was basic energy work. But it served as a reminder, even as I saw Jasra perform the preliminary gestures to a dangerous spell purely as a feint, bringing her near enough to Jurt to trip him, pushing him backward down the stair.

Not Art. Whoever enjoyed the luxury of living near and utilizing a power source such as this would doubtless get very sloppy as time went on, only using the basic frames of spells as guides, running rivers of power through them. One untutored, or extremely lazy, might possibly even dispense with that much after a time and play directly with the raw forces, a kind of shamanism, as opposed to the Higher Magic's purity—like that of a balanced equation—producing a maximum effect from a minimum of effort.

Jasra knew this. I could tell she'd received formal training somewhere along the line. That much was to the good anyway, I decided as I parried another ball of fire and moved to my left.

I began descending the stair—sideways—never taking my gaze off Mask. I was ready to defend or to strike in an instant.

The railing began to glow before me, then it burst into flame. I retreated a pace and continued my descent. Hardly worth wasting a spell to douse it. It was obviously meant for show rather than damage. . . .

Well. . . .

There was another possibility, I realized then, as I saw that Mask was simply watching me, was making no move to throw anything else in my direction.

It could also be a test. Mask might simply be attempting to discover whether I was limited to whatever spells I had brought with me—or whether I had learned to tap the power source here directly and would shortly be slugging things out with him as Jurt and Jasra were now obviously preparing to do. Good. Let him wonder. A finite number of spells against a near-limitless source of energy?

Jurt suddenly appeared upon a windowsill, high and to my left. He had time only for a brief frown before a curtain of fire was rung down upon him. Both he and the curtain were gone a moment later, and I heard Jasra's laughter and his curse, followed by a crashing noise off to the other side of the chamber.

As I moved to descend another step, the stairway faded from view. Suspecting illusion, I continued the slow downward movement of my foot. I encountered nothing, though, and finally extended my stride to pass over the gap and on down to the next stair. It also vanished, however, as I shifted my weight. There came a chuckle from Mask as I turned my movement into a leap to avoid the area. Once I was committed to jumping, the stairs winked out one by one as I passed over them.

I was certain Mask's thinking must be that if I had a handle on the local power, reflex would cause me to betray that connection here. And if I didn't it might still cause me to waste an escape spell.

But I judged the distance to the now-visible floor. If no more stairs vanished I might be able to catch a handhold on the next one, hang a moment, then drop. That would be perfectly safe. And if I missed, or if another stair vanished . . . I still felt I would land reasonably intact. Better to use an entirely different sort of spell on the way down.

I caught the rearward edge of the farthest stair, dangled and dropped, turning my body and speaking the words of a spell I call the Falling Wall.

The fountain shuddered. The fires sloshed and splashed, overflowing the basin on the side nearest Mask. And then Mask himself was thrown backward to the floor as my spell continued its course of descent.

Mask's arms rose before him as his body seemed to sop up the swirling glow, his hands to expel it. There was a bright arc between his hands, then a shieldlike dome. He held it above him, warding off the final collapsive force of my spell. I was already moving quickly in his direction. Even as I did so, Jurt appeared before me, standing on the far lip of the fountain just above Mask, glaring at me. Before I could draw my blade, throw Frakir, or utter

another spell, however, the fountain welled up, a great
wave toppling Jurt from its side, sending him sprawling
upon the floor, washing him past Mask and across the
chamber toward the foot of the other stair, down which
I now saw that Jasra was slowly descending.

"It means nothing to be able to transport yourself
anywhere," I heard her say, "if you are a fool in all
places."

Jurt snarled and sprang to his feet. Then he looked
upward, past Jasra. . . .

"You, too, brother?" he said.

"I am here to preserve your life, if at all possible," I
heard Mandor reply. "I would suggest you return with
me now—"

Jurt cried out—no recognizable words, just an animal-
like bleat. Then, "I do not need your patronage!" he
screamed. "And you are the fool, to trust Merlin! You
stand between him and a kingdom!"

A series of glowing circles drifted like glowing smoke
rings from between Jasra's hands, dropping as if to settle
about his body. Jurt immediately vanished, though
moments later I heard him shouting to Mandor from a
different direction.

I continued to advance upon Mask, who had guarded
successfully against my Falling Wall and was now beginning to rise. I spoke the words of the Icy Path, and his
feet went out from beneath him. Yes, I was going to
throw a finite number of spells against his power source.
I call it confidence. Mask had power. I had a plan, and
the means to execute it.

A flagstone tore itself loose from the floor, turned into
a cloud of gravel amid a grating, crunching noise, then
flew toward me like a charge of shot. I spoke the words
of the Net and gestured.

All of the fragments were collected before they could
reach me. Then I dumped them upon Mask, who was still
struggling to rise.

"Do you realize that I still don't know why we're fighting?" I said. "This was your idea. I can still—"

For the moment, Mask had given up on trying to rise. He had placed his left hand in a simmering puddle of light and had extended his right, palm toward me. The puddle vanished, and a shower of fire emerged from the right hand and sped at me, like drops from a lawn sprinkler. I was ready for this, though. If the Fount could contain the fire, then it had to be insulated against it.

I threw myself flat on the other side of the dark structure, using its base as a shield.

"It is likely one of us is going to die," I called out, "since we are not pulling our punches. Either way, I won't have a chance to ask you later: What's your bitch? What am I to you?"

The only reply was a chuckling sound from the other side of the Fount, as the floor began to move beneath me.

From somewhere off to my right, near the foot of the undamaged stair, I heard Jurt say, "A fool in all places? What about close quarters?" and I looked up in time to see him appear before Jasra and seize hold of her.

A moment later he screamed, as Jasra lowered her head and her lips touched his forearm. She pushed him away then, and he fell down the remaining steps, landing stiffly, not moving.

I crept to the right of the Fount, over the sharp edges of the broken flooring, which jiggled and sawed at me within the matrix of Mask's power.

"Jurt is out of it," I commented, "and you stand alone now, Mask, against the three of us. Call it quits, and I'll see that you go on living."

"Three of you," came that flat, distorted voice. "You admit that you cannot beat me without help?"

" 'Beat'?" I said. "Perhaps you consider it a game. I do not. I will not be bound by any rules you choose to recognize. Call it quits or I'll kill you, with or without help, any way I can."

A dark object suddenly appeared overhead, and I rolled

back away from the Fount as it came to rest in the basin. It was Jurt. Unable to move normally because of the paralytic effect of Jasra's bite, he had trumped away from the foot of the stair and into the Fount.

"You have your friends, Lord of Chaos, and I have mine," Mask replied, as Jurt moaned softly and began to glow.

Suddenly Mask went spinning into the air, as I heard the flooring shatter. The Fount itself died down, grew weaker, as a flaming tower twisted ceilingward, rising from a new opening in the floor, bearing Mask with it on the crest of its golden plume.

"And enemies," Jasra stated, moving nearer.

Mask spread his arms and legs and wheeled slowly through the middle air, suddenly in control of his trajectory. I got to my feet and backed away from the Fount. I'm seldom at my best at centers of geological catastrophes.

A rushing, rumbling sound now came from the doubled fountain, and a high-pitched, sourceless-seeming note accompanied it. A small wind sighed among the rafters. The tower of fire atop which Mask rode continued its slow spiraling, and the spray in the lowered fountain began a similar movement. Jurt stirred, moaned, raised his right arm.

"And enemies," Mask acknowledged, beginning a series of gestures I recognized immediately because I'd spent a lot of time figuring them out.

"Jasra!" I cried. "Watch out for Sharu!"

Jasra took three quick steps to her left and smiled. Something very much like lightning then fell from the rafters, blackening the area she had just departed.

"He always starts with a lightning stroke," she explained. "He's very predictable."

She spun once and vanished redly, with a sound like breaking glass.

I looked immediately to where the old man had stood, RINALDO carved upon his right leg. He was leaning against the wall now, one hand to his forehead, the other implementing a simple but powerful shielding spell.

I was about to scream for Mandor to take the old boy out, when Mask hit me with a Klaxon spell which temporarily deafened me while bursting blood vessels in my nose.

Dripping, I dove and rolled, interposing the now-rising Jurt between myself and the sorcerer in the air. Jurt actually appeared to be throwing off the effects of Jasra's bite. So I drove my fist into his stomach as I rose and turned him into an even better position to serve as my shield. A mistake. I received a jolt from his body, not unlike a nasty electrical shock, and he even managed a brief laugh as I fell.

"He's all yours," I heard him gasp then.

From the corner of my eye, I saw where Jasra and Sharu Garrul stood, each of them seemingly holding one end of a great long piece of macramé work woven of cables. The lines were pulsing and changing colors, and I knew they represented forces rather than material objects, visible only by virtue of the Logrus Sight, under which I continued to operate. The pulse increased in tempo, and both sank slowly to their knees, arms still extended, faces glistening. A quick word, a gesture, and I could break that balance. Unfortunately, I had problems of my own just then. Mask was swooping toward me like some huge insect—expressionless, shimmering, deadly. A succession of brittle snapping sounds occurred within the front wall of the Keep, where a series of jagged cracks raced downward like black lightning. I was aware of falling dust beyond the spiraling lights, of the growling and the whining sounds—faint now within my ringing ears—of the continuing vibration of the floor beneath my half-numbed legs. But that was all right. I raised my left hand as my right slid within my cloak.

A fiery blade appeared in Mask's right hand. I did not stir, but waited a second longer before speaking the guide words to my Fantasia-for-Six-Acetylene-Torches spell as

I snapped my forearm back to cover my eyes and rolled to the side.

The stroke missed me, passing through broken stone. Mask's left arm fell across my chest, however, elbow connecting with my lower ribs. I did not stop to assess damages, though, as I heard the sword of fire crackle and come free of the stone. And so, turning, I struck with my own more mundane dagger of steel, driving its full length up into Mask's left kidney.

There followed a scream as the sorcerer stiffened and slumped beside me. Almost immediately thereafter I was kicked with considerable force behind my right hip. I twisted away and another blow landed upon my right shoulder. I am sure it was aimed for my head. As I covered my neck and temples and rolled away, I heard Jurt's voice, cursing.

Drawing my longer blade, I rose to my feet, and my gaze met Jurt's. He was rising at the same time, and he held Mask cradled in his arms.

"Later," he said to me, and he vanished, bearing the body away with him. The blue mask remained on the floor, near to a long smear of blood.

Jasra and Sharu were still facing each other from kneeling positions, panting, bodies completely drenched, their life forces twisting about each other like mating serpents.

Then, like a surfacing fish, Jurt appeared within the tower of forces beyond the Fount. Even as Mandor hurled two of his spheres—which seemed to grow in size as they fled down the chamber, to crash into the Fount and reduce it to rubble—I saw what I believed I would never see again.

As the reverberation of the Fount's collapse spread and the groaning and grinding within the walls was replaced by a snapping and swaying, and dust, gravel and timbers fell about me, I was moving forward, skirting the wreckage, sidestepping new geysers and rivulets of glowing forces, cloak raised to protect my face, blade extended.

Jurt cursed me roundly as I came on. Then, "Pleased, brother? Pleased?" he said. "May death be the only peace between us."

But I ignored the predictable sentiment, for I had to get a better look at what I thought I had seen moments before. I leaped over a piece of broken masonry and beheld the fallen sorcerer's face within the flames, head cradled against his shoulder.

"Julia!" I cried.

But they vanished even as I moved forward, and I knew it was time for me to do the same.

Turning, I fled through the fire.